LET'S PLAY MAKE-BELIEVE

JAMES PATTERSON

WITH *JAMES O. BORN*

BOOK**SHOTS**

1 3 5 7 9 10 8 6 4 2

BookShots
20 Vauxhall Bridge Road
London SW1V 2SA

BookShots is part of the Penguin Random House
group of companies whose addresses can be found at
global.penguinrandomhouse.com

 Penguin
Random House
UK

· First published by BookShots in 2016

www.penguin.co.uk

A CIP catalogue record for this book is available from the British Library.

ISBN 9781786530394

Printed and bound in Great Britain by Clays Ltd, St Ives Plc

Penguin Random House is committed to a sustainable future
for our business, our readers and our planet. This book is made
from Forest Stewardship Council® certified paper.

LET'S PLAY
MAKE-BELIEVE

PROLOGUE

THE YOUNG REPORTER TRIED to keep her eyes on the camera as it tracked past her to the mansion facing South Ocean Boulevard and the Atlantic on the island of Palm Beach. She thought back to all her journalism and broadcast classes and tried to keep calm. Even with that effort, her voice cracked when the studio anchors cut to her live.

She said, "I am here in the town of Palm Beach as the police try to sort out what has occurred at this South Ocean residence. We know that at least one person has been shot to death, and the killer is believed to be still inside, possibly with a hostage." The young reporter threw in a few improvised lines, then hit the points the producers wanted her to make. "Police have closed this section of South Ocean, and early-morning traffic is backing up as far as the Southern Boulevard Bridge, as we wait to hear exactly what has led to the tense standoff with police on the island of Palm Beach."

Someone off-camera was directing her to step to the side so that the early-morning sun didn't reflect off the lens. As the camera panned to follow the young reporter, there was a growing crowd of neighbors gawking at the scene. Nothing like this had ever happened east of the intracoastal. Police activity of this nature was much more common in West Palm Beach or Riviera Beach. Most of the locals thought Palm Beach was immune to serious crime.

The reporter motioned for the camera to focus back on her and said, "We've heard reports that the town police chief has asked for assistance from the Palm Beach County Sheriff's Office in case they have to make a forced entry into the house."

In the background, near the front of the house, a police officer started to speak into a megaphone. The reporter stopped talking so the camera operators could pick up the audio and show the police officer crouched behind a cruiser.

"Martin Hawking, come out of the front door with your hands up and empty. No one will hurt you if you do it now." There was about a twenty-second break. Then the police officer said, "Come out right now, Mr. Hawking."

CHAPTER 1

I SOMEHOW MANAGED TO slide onto a stool at one of the prime high-top tables near the front door of the Palm Beach Grill. From here you could see the bar, get waited on easily, and keep an eye out for anyone of note who wandered through the main entrance. Landing this high-top was close to a miracle on a Friday evening at seven o'clock, when the place was clogged with Palm Beachers. Julie, the sweet and personable maître d', stopped by, and I gave her a hug.

I needed a night out and a few laughs with my friend Lisa Martz. Like me, Lisa was going through a rough divorce, but she'd hit the ground running and never looked back. The whole thing had struck me a little harder, mainly because it had come out of left field. Lisa was happy to be out of her prison, whereas I'd never thought I was in one.

Lisa signaled to the waitress that we needed another round of margaritas.

I laughed and said, "That'll be my third drink tonight! I'll have to run twenty miles to burn it off tomorrow."

Lisa put her hand on my forearm and said in her sweet Alabama accent, "Don't even talk to me about losing weight. You look fabulous. When Brennan asked for a divorce, it was the best thing that ever happened to you. Everything about you has changed. You look like a cover model with those cheekbones and that smile. If you tell me you're a natural blonde, I might have to stab you with a fork right now."

I had no desire to be stabbed, so I kept my mouth shut. I appreciated my friend's attempt to build my confidence. The fact is, I had been going across the bridge and working out at CrossFit in West Palm Beach, as well as jogging on the beach a couple more days a week. My husband, who was six years older than me, had turned forty a few months ago and decided I was too old for him. He may have phrased it differently, but I'm no idiot. It stunned me then and it still stings now. But I was making every effort not to let that loser dictate the rest of my life. As my dad used to say, "Life is tough enough, don't be a dumbass."

Suddenly, Lisa was waving frantically at a guy across the room, who smiled and worked his way toward us. He was about my age and got better-looking with each step. In good shape, a little over six feet tall, he was dressed casually in a simple button-down and a pair of jeans. A nice change from the usual show-offs on Palm Beach.

Lisa said, "Christy, this is my friend Martin Hawking. Marty, this is Christy Moore. Isn't she gorgeous?"

I admit I liked the goofy, shy smile and the slight flush on Marty's face as he took my extended hand. He had a natural warmth that was intriguing. His short, sandy hair was designed for an active man: it required minimum styling. Before I knew it, we were sitting alone as Lisa got on the scent of a recently divorced gynecologist who was having a few drinks at the other end of the bar.

I said, "I'm sorry if Lisa messed up your evening by dumping you here with me while she went off on the hunt."

Marty let out a quick, easy laugh and said, "I have to be completely honest. When I saw the two of you walk in and she stepped up to the bar beside me, I asked if she would introduce us. I know her from working on the addition to her house over on the island."

"Are you a contractor?"

"No, I'm legit."

He made me laugh, even at such an old joke.

"Actually, I'm an architect. That's just a general contractor who doesn't have enough ambition to make any money. What about you? What do you do?"

I wanted to say, *Make poor choices in men;* instead I said, "I'll tell you when I grow up."

"What would you like to do until then?"

I thought about things I did as a kid growing up in New Jersey. My friends and I kept playing the same games but adapted them as we grew older. I said, "I like games." His hand casually fell across mine on the table and he looked me directly in the eye.

"What kind of games?"

I wasn't used to flirting. I felt like I was crushing it after being so out of practice. Instead of telling him about some lame game I liked as a kid, I said, "Maybe you'll get to find out."

I liked being mysterious for once, and this guy seemed nice and was enjoying it. I couldn't ask for much more right about now.

CHAPTER 2

AFTER OUR MARGARITAS AT the Palm Beach Grill, we ended up at the HMF inside the Breakers Hotel. By then we were on our own, and Lisa was firmly attached to the divorced gynecologist. Marty and I just chatted over drinks. We talked about everything. It was easy, light, and fun. I even found myself opening up about my separation and the pending divorce. He told me a little about his own divorce and how his wife had moved to Vero Beach just so they wouldn't run into each other. It was a good plan.

We threw down some specialty drink at HMS that, as near as I could tell, had vodka, some sort of pink fruit juice, and a lot more vodka. Marty thought we were drinking at the same pace, but I was being much more careful.

I thought hard but just couldn't find the right words to tell Marty how much I'd like him to come back to my place. In my whole life, I'd never picked up a man for a one-night stand. It was new and a little bit scary to me, but I'd be lying if I said there wasn't an element of excitement to it as well.

He gazed at me and said, "You have the most beautiful eyes."

"That's just the alcohol talking."

"No, I mean it. All four of them are beautiful." He weaved his head back and forth like someone pretending to be wildly drunk, and it made me laugh out loud.

That was all I needed to screw up the courage to say, "How would you feel about coming back to my place for a nightcap?"

"How far is it?"

I gave him a look. "It's in Belle Glade, about an hour away."

"What?"

"No, Mr. Clueless, it's here in Palm Beach. No one's ever more than ten minutes from their house when they're on this island."

We grabbed a cab back to my temporary residence at the Brazilian Court Hotel. Although Brennan was beating me out on almost everything in the divorce based on some prenuptial agreement I signed when I really believed he loved me, he didn't want the locals to view him as a complete jerk, and he had put me up in a nice apartment inside the hotel. The cost meant nothing to him, and at least I had a base of operations on the island.

No one asked questions at the Brazilian Court, and Allie, a girl from my CrossFit class, was the evening clerk there. She gave me a heads-up whenever she saw Brennan stomping through the lobby to confront me about one thing or another and generally looked after me like women our age usually did.

Once we were in the room, I realized I was still a little tipsy. I had never used that word in my life until I moved to Palm Beach. Everyone was always getting "a little tipsy," no matter how much they'd had to drink, but in this case, I really was just a little tipsy.

The tiny apartment consisted of a living room and a comfortable bedroom, with a bathroom in between. The balcony in the back looked into the thick tropical foliage that rimmed the property, which was about three blocks from the ocean. This was a trendy place to stay, and the bar could get interesting some nights.

Marty took a look around the place and turned to face me. "We could use some music," he said with a slight slur to his words.

The next thing I knew, we were blasting an older Gloria Estefan song through the oversize external speakers for my iPhone. We also managed to make it to the bamboo-framed couch, and started to make out like teenagers. It was fun and I was getting swept up in it. I lost track of time until I heard a rap on the front door. It might've been going on for a while because it just sort of crept into my consciousness past the music and Marty's kisses.

Someone was now pounding on the door.

CHAPTER 3

MARTY REACHED BACK AND shut off the music as I stood and straightened my cocktail dress. He gave me an odd look and scooted to the bedroom. I realized he was doing it for my benefit so no one would ask any embarrassing questions.

A smile crept across my face as I slowly stepped toward the door, giving Marty time to disappear into the rear of the apartment.

I carefully opened the door a crack, to see my friend Allie's face. I could tell something was wrong.

"What's up, Allie?" I said, without slurring any words. The pride had to be written across my face.

She kept her voice low but said, "My God, Christy, you may want to keep it down a little bit with your new friend. We had complaints from downstairs, as well as people on either side of your room. It sounds like a South Beach nightclub in here." Her slight Serbian accent made it a bit hard to understand her.

"What are they gonna do? Call the cops?"

Her smile told me not much was going to happen.

The old me would've been unbelievably embarrassed; instead, there was something liberating about showing off how much fun I was having. After Allie left, but before I could slip back to tell Marty, there was another knock at the door. I thought Allie had come back.

This time I flung the door open to scare my friend, but then I saw that it was two uniformed Palm Beach cops. I recognized one of them from around town. A typical buff, tan, friendly Palm Beach cop.

He said, "Allie told us she spoke to you, but we have to follow up because someone called us directly and made a complaint."

I used a serious tone even though I wanted to laugh. All I said was "I understand."

"Do you?"

"No more loud music."

The tall cop sighed and said, "We've got enough to do."

"Do you? Do you really?" I couldn't help myself.

The cop smiled and shrugged. "Maybe not, but keep it down anyway."

He could've been a jerk, but luckily, Palm Beach cops are known for being polite to residents, and at least for now I was still considered a Palm Beacher.

I headed back to the bedroom and found Marty looking sober and ready to flee.

"What's up? You're not leaving, are you?"

"I heard the cops. I wasn't sure what was going to happen."

"It was nothing. Just a complaint about the noise. You don't have a problem with cops, do you?"

"Cops and I have a great understanding; I don't bother them and they don't bother me. It works out for us all. Especially in a place like this, where they wouldn't like my West Palm Beach address."

I wasn't sure what he was talking about. "Paranoid much?"

When he didn't seem to get it, I gave him a smile and said, "It's fine. I don't need loud music to prove I'm having a good time."

"You're enjoying yourself?"

"Of course I am, aren't you?" I asked. It was the natural concern of the recently separated.

He sat down on the bed and patted the spread next to him.

I stepped back, then jumped high in the air to land next to him on the king-size bed.

"Let the people downstairs bitch about that," I said as the bed made a tremendous thump on the hard wooden floor. We laughed in bed together until we started kissing again and I lost all track of time. I couldn't remember the last time falling asleep had been so entertaining.

The next thing I remember was a bright light in my face. I was thinking, *Who the hell is shining a light at this time of the night?* When I opened my eyes and everything came into focus, I realized it was the next day and that the bright light was shining in everyone's eyes.

Marty's arms were wrapped around me, and he nuzzled my neck. I could tell by his scratchy voice he didn't feel great when he said, "What time is it?"

I looked at the clock on my nightstand. "Jesus, it's two in the afternoon."

This wasn't a game; I'd had one of the best nights of my life. And I was pretty sure Marty had too. It felt like the smile on my face wouldn't come off all day.

CHAPTER 4

THE NEXT TWO WEEKS were a whirlwind, and I saw Marty Hawking all but two nights. We'd made the focus of our relationship amusing ourselves and keeping things exciting. I felt like a teenager with her first boyfriend. Life can be harsh and people can be rude, but when you're in a fresh romance, everything is easier. That was what the last two weeks had been: fun, thrilling, and unexpected in every way. We went to the Palm Beach Improv in CityPlace and rode the Diva Duck through the streets of West Palm Beach right into the intracoastal. It may have been a touristy thing to do, but having Marty with me made it special.

I adored the way Marty was full of life, just like a big kid. He got so much joy from everything and loved to see me smile. Almost as if he lived for my approval. It was such a nice change from my life with Brennan. He was so reserved. Even though I had been swept off my feet the first time I saw him playing polo, I'd never felt this comfortable around him. It even made me wonder if his obvious wealth had played some role in my feelings toward him. Growing up the daughter of a schoolteacher and a UPS deliveryman had left me wondering what it was like to live without any concerns about money. One thing I'd learned was, even with money you have a lot to worry about.

I was discovering that Marty was an educated, funny guy. He seemed to have made enough money but wasn't consumed by it. His parents lived in Delray Beach, or as he said it, *Everyone's parents live in Delray Beach*. And it sounded like Marty regretted not having any kids. I could relate, but that was the last thing on my mind now. I was too enthralled with this carefree relationship that seemed to revolve around enjoying life.

So when he picked me up early one evening in his slightly dinged twelve-year-old BMW, I was open to his idea to take a leisurely ride all the way down to South Beach, which was more than seventy-five miles away.

We were lucky and found a spot in front of Marjory Stoneman Douglas Park, so we walked down the boardwalk, holding hands the whole time. Unlike Palm Beach, this beach was busy with runners, sightseers, and bicyclists crowding the boardwalk. It was an entirely different vibe from home. Everyone here looked happy.

We ended up at a place called Prime 112 on Ocean Drive and munched on appetizers and sipped incredible wine. It was magical. We moved on to our meal and a wonderful bottle of wine paired to our fillets. If Dwyane Wade or Khloé Kardashian had walked through the tony restaurant, I wouldn't have been surprised.

It was nice to see Marty enjoying himself and acting so relaxed, until our waiter, Diego, brought the bill. In my time with Brennan,

I'd rarely had to worry about the cost of things. It was so different from how I'd grown up. When I saw the look on Marty's face, I had to ask, "What's wrong, babe?"

He showed me the bill, and I saw that it was something over a thousand bucks. For some reason the whole idea started to make me giggle. That in itself struck me as funny and I started to laugh out loud.

That got Marty laughing too. I don't know what it is about a man who laughs easily, but there is almost nothing as attractive to me.

I reached for my purse, and he said, "No. No way. I was the one who dragged you down here and insisted on the most expensive wine." Then he gave me that crazy smile and said, "You ready to play another game?"

"Anything you want."

He pulled two hundred dollars out of his wallet, and when Diego walked by he held it up and said, "I want to make sure you get your tip in cash. No one likes to declare what they earned in tips." Diego smiled and thanked us both, kissing my hand like the South American gentleman he was.

Then Marty said to me, "We're going to make believe we left a card to cover our outrageously expensive meal. Is that okay with you?"

Maybe if he hadn't tipped Diego, I would've been more hesitant. Instead, a tremor of excitement ran through me. "You don't think we'll get caught?"

"Diego got his tip, and he's happy. We'll be blocks away before he even realizes it." Marty reached into his pocket, pulled out his keys, and slipped off his car key, leaving three keys on a ring on top of the bill. "That'll make it look like we're coming back."

"Don't you need your keys?"

"I've got extra keys, and it won't cost me a grand to replace them."

I got the idea that Marty had done stuff like this before.

We stood up from the table, and my heart was pounding. I wasn't sure what the criminal charge would be, but I knew it had to be a felony. This was one thousand dollars we were walking away from. Marty looked casual and unconcerned as he gave me a wink and then reached out to take my hand. Slowly, we turned and looked along our path toward the front door. *Shit.* The manager stood there, chatting with a couple of the waiters, including Diego. Marty took one step that way while I held firm.

"That's crazy. A suicide move," I said in a low voice.

"It's bold and dramatic." He gave me a smile that somehow set me at ease.

I had a better idea. I pulled him back toward the table and around the partition that concealed the way toward the bathrooms. There was another door at the end of the hallway. It led to the little outdoor dining area, where one waitress, who appeared to be thirteen years old, was wandering around. Taking the right angle, with the right pace, we could step through the patio area and over the velvet rope and be only a few feet from freedom. The question was, would the manager and Diego figure out what was going on if they saw us?

We had to do something. I tugged on Marty's hand and pulled him along the corridor. I turned to him and said, "Last chance to pay or use the bathroom. Do you want to do either?"

"Hell, no, I'm an outlaw. I'm with you all the way."

I pushed open the door and was relieved to see there were only two couples on the patio. We wouldn't have to awkwardly step past anyone. The waitress looked up and smiled, eager to have someone else in her section. I just shrugged like we'd walked through the wrong door and then turned quickly to my left, stepping over the rope that sealed off the area as Marty followed me. We took a few steps down the sidewalk and then heard a man's voice shout.

"Wait!"

The manager had seen us.

My impulse was to freeze in place and come up with an excuse, like we were going out to get money from the car. But Marty took off at a sprint and I followed. The CrossFit classes came in handy as we shot north toward Second Street. Just as we turned the corner, I looked over my shoulder and saw the manager and Diego on the sidewalk coming after us.

I said, "We should probably get to the car. We can outrun them easily, but I doubt they'll be happy about us walking out on the bill. They'll have the cops down here looking for us in a few minutes."

Before I knew it, I'd lost any fear and was laughing as we trotted along the sidewalk toward the park, where the car was waiting for us.

I couldn't believe how this guy had brought me out of my shell. I loved that he was so unpredictable and had an edge to him. I never would've thought a respected architect would act like a teenager and do something like dine and dash. This was the most excitement I'd experienced in a long time. Definitely since I'd been locked in this nasty divorce. I'd had no idea life could be this much fun again.

CHAPTER 5

WE DECIDED TO TAKE the long way back to Palm Beach and drove north on the oceanfront US Highway A1A, having to make several detours around inlets, but once we were back in Palm Beach County, it was a steady, comfortable ride with a cool ocean breeze in our faces. The night was beautiful, and Marty seemed to be opening up more and more.

For the first time since we'd met, he started to talk in detail about his divorce. I hadn't wanted to pry, but I was curious. Every divorce has its own story, and it's told by two different people, but in this case, I believed everything Marty said.

Marty changed his voice in an effort to imitate his ex-wife. It wasn't like a comedian who just raises his pitch; Marty actually sounded like an annoyed woman. In his odd falsetto, he said, "Marty, I'm going to need an extra twelve hundred dollars for the trainer this month so I can learn how to properly work my arms. Marty, I'm going to New York this weekend to go shopping with my girlfriends, have you paid off the credit card from last month yet? Marty, why haven't you designed any skyscrapers like John

Nelson, a boy I grew up with whose second major building is going up in Seattle?"

All I could say to him was "I'm sorry, babe. It sounds like you're better off without her. What happened to finally end it?"

He kept his eyes on the road as he spoke. "There's really not much to tell. She fell for an AC contractor. You know how women love air-conditioning." He let out a laugh. "Some tall, goofy guy from Boca Raton. I think he was originally from New Hampshire, and whatever he had, she wanted. The hell of it is, I like him. He's a funny guy. And as much as I try to stay away from both of them, I hear different rumors. Most of them come from the contractors who use me as an architect. I heard he's taking jobs up in Vero just so he can see her and keep his own wife in the dark."

"He's married?"

"Someone's got to be doing the cheating. I read some stat that claimed fifty percent of married men cheat. That means they've got to be finding an equal number of women to cheat with."

"Does that make it harder for you?"

"That she cheated on me? Yeah, it hurt. The fact that we had no kids made the divorce work its way through the system quickly. No-fault. That's all I kept hearing. It's a great idea until you realize your ex-wife gets nearly half of your earnings for the next eight years. It's brutal. Now I live in a rented condo in downtown West Palm and work my ass off just to stay afloat."

"I hope you realize you don't have to spend money just to impress me."

"I'm having a hard time spending enough money just to keep

eating. I figured you were impressed with my sexual skills." That sly smile of his made anything he said adorable.

I leaned across the seat and gave him a kiss on the cheek. Then I couldn't help but bite his earlobe.

Somehow I couldn't resist asking, "What's your ex-wife's name?"

"Teal. I swear to God my ex-wife is named Teal."

That made us both laugh.

Marty said, "She told me she'd always supported me emotionally when I was working. She said I only wanted her happy, in shape, and at home. Then, at the last court proceeding, she said, 'Now I *am* happy, in shape, and at home, and you gotta pay for it awhile longer.'"

Marty took a moment to gather himself. "You know what else she told me?"

"No, what?"

"She told me I should meet someone, I'd feel better." He took his eyes off the road to look at me. "You know what?"

"What?"

"She was right." He had to pull the car to the narrow shoulder of the road in Highland Beach just to kiss me the way he wanted to.

CHAPTER 6

ONCE WE WERE PAST the Lake Worth beach and still heading north on A1A, I told Marty to slow down just a little. I pointed out all the local landmarks I knew so well: the tennis courts at Phipps Park; the condos on Sloan's Curve; and the big houses that sat just off the road, whose residents I named for Marty.

When we were north of the Bath and Tennis Club and clear of Donald Trump's Mar-a-Lago, I had Marty park in one of the spots next to a tiny beach bungalow, more like a cabana, on the beach side of South Ocean. I knew there was no one inside. It was only used occasionally, and even then, just as a way to shower off after swimming in the ocean. I pointed across the street to a mansion that looked like it was surrounded by a golf course.

"See that castle over there? Twenty thousand, two hundred twenty-seven square feet. I've measured it. To the inch. That used to be *my* house. That's where I lived and planned to stay the rest of my life. I loved that place. And my dick of a husband took it away."

"I've heard about your husband. Everyone on the island knows Brennan Moore."

"Don't get me started on that guy." Then, without meaning to, I launched into my own imitation. I tried to put on that irritating, fake accent, as if he had gone to Yale. "This just isn't working out, Christy, dear. I think it's best we go our separate ways." Then I returned to my own voice, trying to keep the bitterness out of it without much success. "That was it. No emotion, no anger. Just his assessment of what was going on and how he intended to correct it. Of course he was bold, because he knew he had a prenup and could lock me out of most of his assets. Not to mention, he had the best attorncys, who I'm sure were ready for this for some time before he said anything to me."

"How's it make you feel now to look up at that house?"

"Angry. Really, really fucking angry." I thought it was best if I didn't go on. I wasn't proud of this side of me. But the fact was, I didn't deserve to be in this position. I was a good wife who'd never even thought about straying and always put Brennan's interests first. I thought that was what couples did. That each wanted the other to be happier than them. Now I was in the real world and I knew that kind of thinking was some part of a fantasy life.

I barely responded when Marty slipped his arm around me to give me a supportive hug. All I could think of was the Italian marble I'd picked out and the true craftsman I'd hired to lay it, and the bamboo wallpaper that set off the study from the rest of the house. That place was mine, and it had been stolen from me.

CHAPTER 7

IT WAS A SHORT ride back to the Brazilian Court, and Marty was in an odd mood that I couldn't decipher. He was quiet and perhaps sullen but clearly deep in thought. I hadn't meant to upset him by showing him the house I used to live in. Maybe he was bothered by the fact that he couldn't pay the dinner bill. All I really wanted to do was make him feel better. I wanted to see that smile. He had one of those smiles that was so sincere it was infectious. It was like a drug, and I needed a fix.

We had a glass of wine from a bottle I had been saving. Then he pulled out a little multicolored pill and said, "Should we try something really wild?"

"What is that? Is it dangerous?" My experience with drugs consisted of trying pot a couple of times in college and hearing stories about some of my friends using cocaine.

Marty said, "It's a new version of Ecstasy that's supposed to completely break down your inhibitions. It's almost like it relieves you of responsibility for your actions. But it keeps you focused and sane. It might be just what we need to take a step further away from our divorces."

I thought about it for a minute, considering what could go wrong. Then, without saying anything, I snatched the pill out of Marty's hand and broke it in half. I didn't wait or think about it again as I popped my half of the pill into my mouth and took a big gulp of wine.

A smile spread across his face as he did the same thing. He reached into his pocket and pulled out another pill as he said, "I have a few of them."

Before long we were back on our favorite couch, making out. The music coming from my speaker system seemed to form colors in the room. It felt wild and natural at the same time.

The pill didn't seem to affect my judgment, just my perception of sight, sound, and touch. The feeling of Marty's hands across my neck and bare shoulders made me shudder with excitement. I could tell I was having the same effect on him when I slipped off his shirt and undid his belt.

That's when there was a knock at the door. A tap at first, then a little louder, until it turned into a good, solid pounding that indicated it was an official visit and not just someone coming by to say hello.

Marty slipped his shirt back on as I stepped to the door and opened it a crack. Once again Allie was standing a few feet from the door with her hands on her hips like she was a schoolmarm about to deliver a lecture. Her long, dark hair was in a loose ponytail, and her pretty, tan face couldn't hide her smile, despite her annoyance. This time I invited her in and introduced her to Marty.

Before she could say anything, I had a glass of wine in her hand.

She sat down on one of the bamboo chairs that matched the couch and said, "I'm trying to head off trouble, Christy. I just got off duty and thought it was best if I came up to tell you we had another complaint about noise. Management is thinking about telling you to find another place to live. I'd hate to see that happen."

Even as she spoke, I realized I was just focusing on the way her mouth moved. She was gorgeous. Even the dowdy hotel uniform couldn't hide her curvy body. The combination of wine and Ecstasy had really done a number on me. I wish I could say I didn't like it, but it was so new and exciting.

After a few minutes, Allie picked up on it and said, "What's with you two? Are you high?"

Marty showed her the pill, and my giggle pretty much explained what was going on. Allie simply reached across and plucked the pill from Marty's hand and popped it into her mouth. I was shocked and pleased at the same time. Now, this was a party.

Before any of us could change our minds, we were all scampering to the bedroom and losing our clothes along the way. The bed felt like it was swallowing us whole as Marty and Allie planted themselves on either side of me. Maybe I had been a good girl for too long. This was the kind of night I had fantasized about but had never told anyone.

It really was fun being a bad girl once in a while.

CHAPTER 8

THE NEXT MORNING I was surprised to find myself alone in bed. Somewhere in my foggy brain I realized Allie had left in the middle of the night, but that didn't explain Marty's absence. For just a moment, it flashed in my head that he had left with her. But that wasn't how I recalled it. The night was a wild, sweaty, and exhilarating blur. I wasn't sure I could give any details if I was asked to. But I didn't regret it. Not for a moment. I just hoped it wouldn't be awkward with Allie. Then again, thinking about some of the things she'd done in bed made me realize she wasn't much for feeling awkward. And that last night hadn't been her first time in a threesome. Live and learn.

I sat up in bed, and it took a moment for my vision to catch up with me. I slipped into a sundress and looked through the apartment, trying to figure out if Marty had left a note or any clue about where he had gone. Then I noticed his wallet and keys on the desk in the living room. He had made coffee for me as well. I gladly took a cup and sipped it as I sat back on the couch and tried to piece together everything that had happened the night before. I had gone from feeling angry about the divorce and losing my house to the wild delight of a new experience that I would never get to brag about. Not bad for a Wednesday.

A few minutes later, Marty came through the door wearing his short swim trunks and an old T-shirt with the logo completely faded. He looked great. He was trim and tan and had just enough muscles to prove he wasn't a slacker. Every inch of him was covered in sweat.

I was surprised how relieved I was to see him. I couldn't explain the doubts I'd had when he wasn't in bed with me when I woke up. And I'm typically not that insecure.

"You were quite a ninja leaving this morning. I had no idea where you went."

He grabbed his left foot and held it behind his back to stretch his quadriceps as he said, "You looked so peaceful when I woke up that I slipped out and used the workout clothes you let me keep here. I went for a run along the public beach and kept heading south, all the way to your former house. In the daylight, it's even more spectacular. I could see that even the bungalow on the beach was beautiful. Something about running on the deserted beach and seeing that big house really pissed me off. As badly as I was treated by my ex, I feel like you were treated worse."

Obviously I agreed with him, but I didn't want to sound vindictive or petty. I just gave him a quick kiss on the cheek to show my appreciation. But the look in his eyes told me there was more to what he was saying. Seeing that house had sparked something in Marty. He wasn't exactly who I'd thought he was when I first met him. And I wasn't sure if that was good or bad.

CHAPTER 9

THERE WAS NO WAY I could risk the scandal of a dine-and-dash at a local restaurant, so when the bill came at Charley's Crab, I snatched it right out of Marty's hand. We'd had lunch and only had a few cocktails. I hadn't been a midday drinker since I was in college, but it was kind of fun and there was something about doing it with Marty that made it seem okay.

Before I could get to the bottom figure on the bill, Marty had grabbed it back and handed his American Express card to the waitress.

I didn't want money to become a problem between us, so I said, "We don't have to keep eating at fancy restaurants every day. I'm a simple girl from Jersey. A sub or a hot dog can keep me filled up for a long time." I hadn't meant it as a double entendre, but the smile on his face told me that was how he took it. A typical guy. But in his case, he was so good-natured that anything I said to make him smile made me happy.

Marty said, "It's fine, I have jobs lined up back to back that will carry me through next summer. I may not be designing the next New York library or be considered the Addison Mizner of my generation, but at least I have a good reputation. And it's nice to have the money coming in." He paused for a moment, then added, "Teal is happy about it too."

I caught the bitterness in his voice. Recently, I'd been trying to judge if he was getting over his ex-wife and the circumstances of his divorce, or if he was focusing on them more. It was hard to tell. In a way it made him more human, like a regular guy. He wasn't flawless, even though I found him engaging and caring.

As we were standing by the covered front entrance to Charley's Crab, I looked up and was shocked to see Brennan driving by us on Ocean Boulevard in his Jaguar convertible. It was the blue one that I'd picked out for him. I couldn't keep a "son of a bitch" from coming out of my mouth.

Marty looked up quickly and said, "What's wrong?"

I nodded toward the Jag and said, "There's Brennan looking like he owns the world." And he did. It looked like he should be wearing a commodore's cap. Then he did the worst thing I could imagine him doing. It cut me like a knife and left me shaking.

He waved to me.

Not a nasty wave. Not a condescending wave. Just a casual raising of his right hand like we were old acquaintances passing on the street. Like I meant nothing to him. Not only was he over me, it was like I had never existed.

I couldn't let Marty see how this was affecting me, so I pretended to sneeze and put my hands over my face.

Marty was too smart for that. He slid an arm around my shoulder and said, "Let's find a place to sit back and talk for a while."

CHAPTER 10

WE WALKED ACROSS THE street to the public beach and found a park bench on the south end. It was a breezy day and the sun was behind us as we looked out over the choppy Atlantic. A lot of people say the Palm Beach public beach is the least-enticing beach in Florida. Parking is expensive and the locals clearly don't want people visiting from off the island, but our comfortable bench, just off the road, provided a vista most people can only see in magazines.

Marty put his arm around me and didn't say a word. He didn't try to solve my problems or analyze me or give me advice. We just sat quietly, and I found my head rolling onto his shoulder. It was exactly what I needed. Before I knew it, I started to talk. I talked about Brennan and our marriage for maybe the first time.

When people hear you're going through a divorce, it's almost like you have some communicable disease. They stay at arm's length and let you know they're still your friends, but that this is probably something you should get through on your own.

Not Marty. He just listened.

I said, "Brennan was so dashing the first time I ever saw him. He was playing polo in Wellington and I was there with a girlfriend. He looked like a knight sweeping through the pack and swinging his mallet, or club, or whatever they call that thing that hits the ball. It was almost like a dream, it was so perfect. And he was charming. I mean actually charming, not faking it. He had an accent like a yacht club member on Martha's Vineyard, but he was also funny and extraordinarily polite. A sense of humor and good manners go a long way with most women.

"Until about our third date, I hadn't even known he'd been married before. They had been college sweethearts, and it sounded like she hurt him pretty badly. At least that's how I interpreted it. I never heard many specific details, except when he'd tell me she never made him feel like I did. What a load of shit."

Marty didn't seem fazed at all by my rambling as we both watched the few families on the beach build sand castles or run through the shallow water along the shore.

"Brennan proposed to me after six months. Two days before the wedding, he said his father insisted on him signing a prenup with me. He assured me it was no big deal, but the family wanted to protect the assets that provided the income for him. I didn't care about money. I really still don't. At least not that much. Anyway, I never even bothered to consult an attorney. All I wanted was to be his wife, maybe have a few kids, and live with this dream husband. I signed the prenup. Ugh. What a rookie mistake."

Marty said, "You didn't talk to any of your friends about it?"

"None of them had any experience with prenups. They were all married to teachers, insurance agents, or firemen." I wiped a tear from my eye and regained my composure. I hated that Brennan still got to me like this. Then I said, "He never really kept any promises. We were going to travel, have a kid, be a family. He never even took me to Disney World like I wanted. He said there was no time. It was Disney World, for God's sake. Was that too much to ask? My parents couldn't afford a trip from Jersey when I was little, and my husband didn't have time for fun. I've still never been to the Magic Kingdom." I looked out at the ocean in an effort to hide my emotions. Marty had done nothing to deserve this kind of baggage.

After a long silence Marty said, "What happened in the end? I mean, why'd you guys break up?"

"Maybe he wanted a younger woman, but I think the real reason is that he just got bored with me. Then he threw me out on the street. I was so stunned, I barely made a squeak."

Marty kissed me. "That's where he's wrong. You are anything but boring. You've revived me."

That was exactly what I needed to hear him say.

CHAPTER 11

OVER THE NEXT FEW days, Marty and I got in the habit of walking the beach and talking. We always started from the north end of the public beach and strolled south, right past my former house. I liked being seen with such a good-looking man. I wanted people to know that my life wasn't over just because someone like Brennan was trying to divorce me. It was simply a lot of fun to be with a guy like Marty, who listened and made me feel wanted. What a change from Brennan.

Some days, I agreed to jog on the beach because I knew Marty preferred the faster pace. I wanted to prove I could keep up with him. It was the competitive streak of a girl raised by a man who had wanted a son. Some days I ran hard on the sand, making my heart race. Marty appreciated the effort. Brennan never would've even noticed.

I wondered why I was trying so hard to please Marty; then I realized just how serious my feelings were for him. He'd rescued me and changed the trajectory of my life, and I was actually happy. It was incredible.

The one thing that seemed to interrupt my joy was when I flashed back to my life with Brennan.

It's hard to explain, but every time I saw the house from the beach, I got a little angrier. I know there are people in the world with much more serious problems. I had my health, a new boyfriend, and a lot more life to live, but it sure would have been nice if that house had been part of my life. I could picture Marty sitting by the pool or working on house plans in the den.

Just when I thought I couldn't get more annoyed, one day we noticed Brennan getting ready to pull out of the driveway. He wasn't in the Jag. The bastard was driving a brand-new Bentley. A black Bentley Mulsanne that seemed to shimmer in the sunlight. He'd bought a more formal car to go with his convertible.

Marty and I were running out on dinner tabs and this son of a bitch had a car for every occasion. Something just wasn't right about it.

Marty said, "What an asshole. Anyone under seventy who drives a Bentley is, by definition, an asshole."

I reached out and gripped his hand. Marty really was on my side. His face was red and he looked like he was ready to burst through the gate next to the bungalow and charge Brennan in his brand-new Bentley.

Marty said, "I could punch that guy in the face."

I stared at Marty, wondering how serious he was. He stepped toward the gate, and I reached out to hold his arm. We watched as Brennan, oblivious to the world as usual, pulled out and drove away in the Bentley.

Marty took a breath and shook his head. "I should welcome you to the club."

"What club?"

"The getting screwed in your divorce club."

His color had already come back, showing off his pleasant tan complexion, and there was a hint of a smile on his face. He looked like he had just been blowing off steam and Brennan was a convenient target.

Then Marty said, "Don't worry, it gets better."

"Really?"

"It did for me."

"How long does it take?"

"It got better as soon as I met you."

I had to kiss this sweet man.

But thinking about the house and Brennan's new car, I did wonder about what, exactly, that jerk deserved. Not just in the divorce, but in life as well.

CHAPTER 12

ON FRIDAY OF THAT week, I saw Brennan again. This time at Family Court in the Palm Beach County Courthouse. Even though Brennan didn't feel like family to me anymore. He gave me a smirk when I walked in with my attorney.

The judge had read both sides' briefs, and I felt confident he'd grant our motion to throw out the prenup.

I listened quietly while the attorneys answered questions about the progress of the divorce and who would be testifying today. All three of Brennan's high-priced attorneys against my cute little mama's boy from Boca Raton, whose mother was my hairdresser and had said he was good and cheap. And that he needed the work.

My attorney shuffled nervously through papers as I looked over at Brennan's crowded table. Brennan was impeccably dressed in one of his many dark Ralph Lauren suits, but hadn't been able to resist the typical Palm Beach touch of a turquoise flowered tic. Not a power tie. He didn't need one.

My chance to testify had finally come. It wasn't in the witness box like I had imagined. The judge instructed me to stand right next to where I was sitting and answer his questions.

The older, dignified man kept looking down at some notes, until finally he said, "Mrs. Moore, has your attorney explained the three main reasons that are grounds for dismissing a prenuptial agreement?"

"Yes, Your Honor."

"And you understand that *duress* means the agreement was presented too close to the date of the marriage, or some similar issue?"

"Yes, Your Honor."

"And *coercion* would be like offering ultimatums, and *fraudulent financial disclosure* explains itself."

"Yes, Your Honor."

The judge nodded. "Very well, let's get started." Now he gave me his full attention and said, "Mrs. Moore, what did you do for a living before your marriage?"

"I was in marketing."

"And do you have a college degree?"

"From Rutgers, yes, sir."

The judge said, "Ah, a Scarlet Knight, very good. I'm from Trenton. We're the only state without a university named after it."

"Yes, sir." I didn't know what else to say. At least he was trying to put me at ease.

"And would you say your income was low, high, or average?"

I kept focusing on breathing and keeping cool. "Average, Your Honor." I paused and added, "To low average."

The judge nodded and wrote down a few notes, and then, in a

very calm and quiet manner, said, "How long before the wedding date was the prenuptial agreement presented to you by Mr. Moore?"

"Two days before the date we had set."

The judge said, "Did Mr. Moore offer any ultimatums? Did he ever say anything like 'If you don't sign this, we're not getting married'?"

This was another important question. I gathered my thoughts and said, "Brennan said his dad needed the agreement signed, and if not, we'd start off our life together broke. I told him I was used to not having any money. He said he wasn't and then just stood silently until I signed the agreement. I later learned that he was really concerned about his own assets."

I stood, trying to hide my smile at having been so concise in showing duress, coercion, and false financial disclosure in my brief exchange with the judge. I had hit this one out of the park.

But then it was Brennan's turn.

CHAPTER 13

THE JUDGE HAD SOME of the same questions about background and how we met. Brennan pointed out that he'd graduated from Georgetown and worked in finance. I guess if you manage your family's hedge fund you are, sort of, working in finance.

Then the judge asked him about the intent behind the prenup.

At that moment, I wished Marty was sitting next to me so I could hold his hand. Also, I wanted him to see firsthand how pompous Brennan was.

Brennan finally got to the meat of his answer. "The intent of the prenuptial agreement was to protect not only my assets, but assets that had come to me through my family. The prenuptial agreement was something I had discussed with my parents and lawyers long before I'd ever met Christy."

"Did you feel you waited too long to present the agreement?"

"No, Your Honor. Not at all. We'd talked about it for months before I presented it to her."

That was a lie, but my lawyer's death grip on my arm told me we'd get a chance to straighten out the record.

The judge said, "Would you still have married Mrs. Moore if she had not signed the agreement?"

This was what I was waiting to hear. This was a question I had been asking myself since Brennan had tossed me out.

Brennan said, "It never came to that, Your Honor. Christy signed immediately. I never had to consider any alternatives. I loved her, Your Honor, but I do have certain responsibilities. I'm glad I didn't have to make that choice."

The judge said, "Do you feel the absence of a prenuptial agreement would have affected the marriage in any way?"

I had never even *thought* about the agreement until Brennan dumped me. So clearly the damn thing had not affected our marriage one bit. At least from my perspective.

Brennan said, "Looking back, Your Honor, I feel Christy might have been more interested in my *lifestyle* than me. And the fact that we're having this hearing confirms that theory." Then he added, "I can't say she ever showed any genuine emotion toward me."

There was no reason for Brennan's last remark. He knew it wasn't true. I'd loved him and thought he loved me.

He just stood there as if he expected applause.

I felt a tear well up in one eye. Why was I crying now? Maybe because not only was it over, but I was realizing that nothing had ever actually existed between us. I was just some kind of trophy for him.

The judge said, "Thank you, Mr. Moore. You may sit down now."

My husband, because he was still my husband, in fact and in the eyes of the law, turned in his chair and looked right at me. When he had my full attention, he winked and gave me a smug smile.

The judge considered everything he'd heard and told the attorneys to hold their questions. Then he looked up and cleared his throat. This was it. He had recognized that I'd signed the agreement under duress, I'd been coerced, and Brennan had presented me with false financial data. I looked at my attorney, who was also smiling. He was optimistic too.

The judge said, "Gentlemen, I have carefully considered your motions on behalf of your clients, and after hearing from both Mr. and Mrs. Moore, I've concluded that Mrs. Moore is a very intelligent, educated woman who signed the agreement willingly, without undue pressure or while under duress; therefore…"

I didn't hear the rest, but then again, I didn't really need to. All I heard was the judge's final comment. "Mrs. Moore's motion to dismiss the prenuptial agreement is denied." He looked up at both tables and said, "Let's start to move this along now, shall we." Then it was over. My best shot at recovering part of my old life had been a failure.

Brennan stood with a broad smile on his face and shook all of his lawyers' hands like he was O. J. Simpson and had just avoided a double murder rap.

I spent the next few moments consoling my attorney, who felt like he had let me down. I wrapped my arm around his shoulder and hugged him. He sniffled and nodded.

As Brennan passed me on his way out of the courtroom, he

stopped and leaned down. "You look great, babe. Sorry about your little motion."

"Why are you doing this? Why humiliate me on top of everything else?"

Brennan just grinned and said, "Because I can, and there isn't a damn thing you can do about it."

CHAPTER 14

OUTSIDE THE COURTHOUSE, MY lawyer said it was all his fault. As I looked at him and his off-the-rack suit and Supercuts haircut, my thick file tucked under his right arm, I realized he had no idea the hearing had been fixed. He'd followed the rules and assumed everyone else would as well. I'd done the same, and look where that had gotten me.

My lawyer said, "I'll keep looking for something we can exploit. But at some point you have to get on with your life. Christy, you're a beautiful woman, and you shouldn't let this experience sour your outlook on love."

That was an easy thing for a father of three who had been married twenty years to say. I gave him a hug and sent him on his way.

That evening Marty had to work, so I sat in my quiet room at the Brazilian Court Hotel and did nothing but search the Internet for legal precedents and articles about situations like mine. I wanted to explore every possible option I had.

That night I barely slept, tossing and turning, my stomach tightening every time I thought about the hearing.

The next day, Marty came by around lunchtime, when I was only barely starting my day. He talked me into taking one of our usual walks along the beach. I was quiet for a while; then, after we had gone a way in the soft sand, he said, "Sorry I didn't sleep over, but I had a ton to do. But because I worked during the night, now I have a few hours to spend with you on a beautiful day like this."

I said, "It's all right. I was on my iPad all night doing legal research anyway." That seemed to catch his attention.

"I thought your attorney was supposed to do that kind of thing for you. Did you at least find anything interesting?"

"A few things." I wasn't sure if I was playing coy or worried about trusting Marty completely. It was easier to make him work for the answers so I could decide what I might say.

Marty said, "A few interesting legal leads? Can you give me a for-instance."

I decided to jump in with both feet. "Did you have a will when you were going through your divorce?"

Marty said, "I had nothing to leave anyone. Teal was getting it all anyway."

"Did you know that if you die without a will, it's called dying *intestate* and generally the spouse is in line to get everything?"

That made Marty stop in his tracks. He even glanced around to make sure no one was near us on the beach, but by now we were blocks from the public beach and there wasn't a soul in sight. He looked right at me and said, "That can't be right. Even in a divorce."

I told him what I had read. "As long as the divorce isn't final, and there is no will, all of the precedents say the spouse is entitled to the estate."

"Aren't wills filed in court?"

"No. They can be held by the attorney, but usually they're just kept right at the home of the deceased. It's convenient and doesn't cost anything. And most people really don't think they're gonna die anytime soon. It's just one of those details that floats by in life."

Marty started walking again and just said, "Really? Good to know. Next time I'm wealthy, I'll make sure to give a will to my attorney just in case. One less thing to worry about." He gave me that adorable smile that made all my troubles melt away. That was a rare quality in a man and something that couldn't be faked. I started to realize just how lucky I'd been to find Marty at this time in my life.

CHAPTER 15

IT TOOK ALMOST A week for me to get back to normal, but Friday afternoon Marty surprised me by showing up at the Brazilian Court, looking like a true Palm Beacher in his linen shirt with a cashmere sweater draped over his shoulders, khakis, and loafers with no socks. His fake Rolex would pass all but the closest of inspections.

As I assessed him spinning in my doorway and looking a little like a model, all he said to me was "Got any plans?"

I let the smile spread across my face as I said, "None at all."

I almost thought he'd take me for another walk along the beach, but he told me to dress up and not expect to be back at the hotel for quite a while. I had no idea what that meant.

We hopped into his BMW and drove across the bridge into the center of downtown West Palm. Traffic was much heavier than it was on the island, and I was curious where we were headed.

He turned onto some side roads, obviously to throw me off and have some fun. The man took his games seriously, and I loved that. Then we found ourselves westbound on Okeechobee once again and crossing over I-95.

Finally I had to ask, "Where are we going?"

His goofy smile was infectious as he said, "You'll see. We're just going to play a game. Are you up for that?"

I could've said *That depends,* but I really was in the mood for something different. I needed to get my head out of my troubles, at least for a little while.

So I grabbed his free hand, which was resting on the gearshift. "Yes."

When Marty pulled in to the Bentley dealer off Okeechobee, I became even more curious. This was a fun game, and I had no idea where it was headed. I knew there had to be some connection to seeing Brennan in his own Bentley the other day, but I was happy to watch the whole thing unfold.

I was in a dress that was more appropriate for an evening event but could pass for business attire at some of the higher-end jewelry stores or any of the shops on Worth Avenue. The Christian Louboutin pumps on my feet weren't the easiest things to walk in, but they made my calves pop, so I had thrown a pair of comfortable shoes into the bag Marty had told me to pack.

I resisted the urge to ask questions and spoil the spontaneity as we walked, hand in hand, through the front door of the dealership and stood next to a dark red Mulsanne. Marty looked through the window of the car and down the hood like he was checking for imperfections. That drew a salesman like chum draws sharks.

We endured the introductions and a few minutes of small talk until the tall salesman, about forty-five, who could've been selling

Mazdas as well as Bentleys, said, "So what, exactly, brings you out here today?"

Marty was very casual as he said, "My wife and I are in the market for a new car, and I thought it was time to seriously consider a Bentley. Brennan Moore recommended you guys."

That line shocked me, but it had the desired effect on the salesman.

"I sold Brennan his Mulsanne, just like the one sitting right here." He patted the hood of the car like it was a racehorse. "Brennan is a great guy, and I'm so happy he recommended us."

The salesman looked at me for some kind of response, but all I could do was mumble, "Yeah, yeah, he's the best."

Marty said, "We see him over on the island quite a bit, and I like the look of his new car. But we usually don't go for long drives."

The whole time, I marveled at Marty's inventive deviousness. I still had no idea what this game was.

Marty said to the salesman, "Although we've considered a Flying Spur, we're seriously looking at a Mercedes across the street at Mercedes-Benz of Palm Beach. I just wanted to show her a couple of Bentleys." Then he turned toward the door and took a few steps.

It was genius. I had never seen anything like it. Immediately the salesman lunged for us, saying, "Wait, wait, you don't want a German car on the island. Bentley is the only way to go."

Marty was masterful. The salesman essentially begged us to take a Flying Spur for a test drive.

Marty remained aloof and said, "I'm not sure driving a few blocks in the car is gonna give me the confidence I need to buy it."

The salesman said, "No problem. All I need is a little information, just your cell phone and maybe your driver's license, and you can take it home overnight and really get a feel for it. We'll even come by and pick it up if you don't like it, or we can complete the paperwork right at your house."

Even though the salesman was a little aggressive, I felt sorry for him. He was standing in front of us like a puppy waiting for a treat.

Marty hesitated and then gave him his cell number.

When the salesman said, "We just need a little bit more information," Marty countered with "I don't have time for paperwork."

Then he looked at me and said, "Let's go." He turned like an impatient Palm Beacher would, and the salesman jumped up with the keys, telling us to just give them a call if we needed anything.

A few minutes later, after we had retrieved a few things from Marty's BMW, we pulled out of the parking lot, but instead of turning east toward Palm Beach, Marty turned west on Okeechobee.

I said, "Where are we going now?"

A satisfied smile popped onto his face as he said, "You'll find out."

I loved this game. We held hands and chatted as he pulled onto the turnpike headed north. I didn't ask any questions. I just enjoyed the ride as we took the turnpike farther north until Marty pulled off onto Osceola Parkway and then off again at an exit just south of Orlando. I had to fight the urge to ask questions, but when he pulled into the Four Seasons right outside Disney World, I couldn't help but show my surprise. Who doesn't want to visit Disney World? I had just told him how Brennan had promised but had never taken me. I threw my arms around Marty's neck and planted a big kiss on his lips.

As we got out of the car I had to tell him, "This game of make-believe is fantastic."

CHAPTER 16

DISNEY WORLD WAS ALL I had dreamed it would be. At least the attractions were, anyway. Somehow, when I was a kid, I'd never calculated how many people were crammed into the park every day. Especially on a beautiful Saturday like this. We managed to make it onto most of the rides, though the longest waits were at Space Mountain and Pirates of the Caribbean. I might have enjoyed a trip to the Magic Kingdom more when I was eleven, but being here today with Marty was really special too. Maybe the most important thing was that I realized how carefully Marty had listened to me and how badly he wanted to see me happy. This guy would do anything for me, and no one had ever made me feel like that before.

Walking hand in hand with Marty made me feel like no matter what choices I had made, I had the right man in my life now. He was just what I needed.

But after lunch my mood started to change. It began with the salesman from the Bentley dealer calling Marty and asking how he liked the car. Marty handled it perfectly, telling the salesman we were still undecided but we'd bring the car back later this afternoon.

As Marty stuffed the phone back into his front pocket, he smiled at me and said, "I just won't answer the phone again until we're about to drop the car off."

The call had brought me back to reality, and my problems were no longer a world away. I started thinking about the court hearing and that pompous ass Brennan. While we were floating in our boat through It's a Small World, I noticed our conversation had turned darker as well.

Out of nowhere Marty said, "Disney makes a fortune separating people from the real world and the ugliness around them."

"Whoa, what brought that on?" The little girl in front of us had been peeking behind the seat since the ride had started. She might not have understood what he was saying, but she picked up on Marty's attitude and quickly twisted around to sit low in her seat, out of sight.

Our conversation drifted back to normal, Magic Kingdom–related topics as we shuffled our way through the Haunted Mansion and Frontierland. Once we landed in comfortable seats and under air-conditioning at the PhilharMagic 3-D, with no one sitting close to us, I acted on the urge to kiss him.

Marty said, "I'm glad you're having a good time. I'm sorry you missed out on Disney for so long, but I'm glad your ex-husband didn't hurt your sense of joy."

"First of all, he's not my ex-husband yet. And he didn't hurt my sense of joy, but he did come close to ruining it. He was never the man I thought he was. It turns out *you* are the man I thought *he* was."

We kissed again, deeply and passionately. I felt Marty's hand around the back of my neck, and I wanted to hold him tight. As the show began and objects came flying at us in 3-D, we continued making out, grabbing at the visual effects before us. I'd never thought I'd enjoy the PhilharMagic 3-D so much.

Somehow I knew Marty was a guy I could depend on. He would protect me, and since he had taken me to Disney World, I knew he just wanted to make me happy. Who could ask for anything more?

CHAPTER 17

I THOUGHT THE SALESMAN was going to kiss Marty when we dropped off the Bentley. He darted out of the showroom and met us in the parking lot.

The salesman blurted out, "I thought you'd—"

Marty was back in character as the annoyed rich guy and said in a sharp tone, "What? You thought we'd what?"

The salesman stammered and said, "F-forgotten us. You just surprised me by keeping the car a little extra. You must have really loved it." He was standing in front of us, almost hopping in place with excitement, like a kid about to open a Christmas present. "What do you think? Will you pull the trigger on it? I can have everything ready for you to sign in just a few minutes."

He was following along in the parking lot as Marty walked toward the back where his car was parked. The salesman didn't even seem to realize he was being led away from his office.

Marty waited until we were right next to his car so we could enjoy the look on the salesman's face when he opened the door of his beat-up BMW. The salesman's expression said it all.

As Marty and I slipped into the car, Marty said, "Think I'll stay with my Beemer for now."

We giggled about it all the way back to Palm Beach.

The night ahead of us ended up being one of the best endings to one of the best weekends of my life. I tried another one of Marty's crazy little pills, and this time we didn't wait for Allie to show up. I called her. And she brought a friend. A tall, very young, and really hot Czech bartender from Café Boulud, the restaurant right in the hotel. He had blond hair and blue eyes, and he eagerly accepted one of Marty's homemade Ecstasy tabs. I couldn't even pronounce his name, which didn't sound like it had any vowels in it, and his accent was thicker than Allie's. But he wasn't here to talk.

Before I knew it, we had our own disco going, with my speakers blaring out dance songs from the eighties on Pandora. We left the music on as each couple started to get more intimate and clothes started to fly onto the floor.

The young bartender looked like he belonged in a Tommy Hilfiger ad, with his flat stomach and ripple of muscles that popped perfectly against his tightie-whities.

Suddenly, I heard a knock on the door. It wasn't like when Allie would tap and then rap a little harder. This was an immediate pounding.

Allie scooted from the couch and said, "I'll get fired if I'm caught in here."

"Me too," added the bartender.

I shut off the music and called out, "Who is it?" Trying to keep my best homemaker's voice.

From outside the door I heard, "Palm Beach Police, Mrs. Moore."

That had an effect on Marty, who sprang up and started toward the bedroom. I said, "You need to stay out here with me this time. These two have to go into the bedroom. They can't be caught in here or they'll lose their jobs."

Marty said, "Leave it to me. They won't get their names." He scrambled to get dressed as I slipped my blouse back on and pulled up a pair of shorts. I opened the door a crack, like I was worried about who was there. It was the same two cops who had crashed our first party. That must have been how they'd known my name.

I opened the door and waved them inside.

Only one of the cops spoke, just like last time. He was tall and handsome, with blond hair and great arms. They strained the sleeves of his polyester uniform.

He glanced around the room and noticed the other clothes, and even I could see the shadows of Allie and the bartender under the door of the bedroom. They weren't particularly discreet.

The cop said, "Looks like you're having quite a party."

Marty smiled and said, "Wanna join in?"

Neither of the cops thought that was very funny, and they got it across with a long, surly look at Marty. That made Marty clear his throat and say, "Just kidding, you guys."

The cop pulled a pad from his back pocket and said, "I'm sorry, Mrs. Moore, but we had another complaint about the noise. I just need to write a quick report about it. If you promise to keep it down, we'll let this one slide too."

"I promise." I was in no mood to deal with the police.

The cop looked at Marty and said, "And your name, sir?"

Marty hesitated. "Why do you need my name?"

"Why don't you want to give me your name?"

"Why *should* I give you my name?"

"Because we were called here on a complaint of noise and you appear to have been contributing to that noise. I think we've been very polite and pleasant during this encounter, but that is going to end if you don't give me your name. Now."

I immediately understood that Marty was distracting the cops from Allie and the bartender, but I also saw how serious the cop was, so I was surprised that Marty stood his ground. He really didn't want to give the cop his name. The whole encounter was kind of thrilling, at least through my drug-enhanced view of it. I just hoped Marty's ploy worked and the cops didn't go to the bedroom and get Allie's and the bartender's names as well.

Finally Marty said, "My name is Martin Hawking." He didn't give the cop any more trouble as he provided his date of birth and address.

On the way out, the cop said, "You guys need to keep it down. Palm Beach goes to bed early and it doesn't like scandals."

Allie peeked out of the bedroom as soon as she heard the door shut, and Marty excused himself to go to the bathroom.

Allie said, "I could hear everything through the door. Your boyfriend just saved our jobs. He's fantastic."

I looked at her and said, "Yes, yes, he is."

CHAPTER 18

THE NEXT MORNING I woke up with Marty's arm draped across me. For a few seconds I panicked, wondering if Allie and the bartender were still in the apartment. I had never experienced that kind of fear in the morning and vowed right then never to take another one of Marty's crazy pills. I'm not saying I regretted it. Everyone needs to get wild once in a while, but things had gone a little too far last night. I wasn't completely clear on what had happened after the cops left.

We knew to keep it quiet, but there was still more drinking, and the bartender had some really potent pot. The night got wilder, and now I vaguely recalled Allie and the bartender slipping out sometime in the early-morning hours.

Marty stirred and I turned in bed, giving him a kiss to wake him up. That put the smile that I wanted to see on his face.

Without prompting, he said, "Maybe we don't need any pharmaceutical help to have fun anymore. I'm not sure I'll ever say the sentence 'It's not really a party until the cops show up' again."

That made me laugh as I rolled onto my back and looked up at the ceiling. It wasn't just the small square footage of the apartment that was such a change from my previous residence; it was the overall feel of everything, from the low ceilings to the tiny bathroom. It immediately got me thinking about my house on South Ocean and the jackass who'd thrown me out of it.

Marty said, "What would you like to do today?"

An idea popped into my head and I just said it out loud: "I have a key to my old house, and I'd like to pay a visit if Brennan isn't there."

"You want to burglarize your old house?"

"Technically, I think we would just be trespassing."

"No, I'm pretty sure you're talking felony."

"Anyway..." I turned to look Marty in the eye and said, "Are you game?"

He shrugged his bare shoulders and said, "Why not? The Palm Beach cops already love me."

That was all there was to it. After a little breakfast, our usual walk on the beach ended up at the beach bungalow across the street from the house. It didn't take long for us, sitting on the beach together, to see Brennan pull out in the Jaguar. He headed south, which meant he was crossing the Southern Boulevard Bridge, and I knew he'd be gone for at least an hour. It isn't worth leaving the island unless you're going to be gone for more than an hour. That was plenty of time.

We had to jump the gate at the beach and cross the street quickly, but then we just walked up the driveway, and I led Marty past the front door and through an unlocked gate into the backyard. The key I had was to the pool house, and as we walked through it, I realized that it was almost twice the size of my current apartment.

We paused for a minute before we stepped through the door that led to one of the rear patio rooms. I listened and didn't hear anyone. Generally, Brennan kept a very small staff, just a housekeeper and a guy who supervised the lawn and pool care. He wasn't here every day.

I also knew that Brennan activated the alarm system only when the house was going to be empty for a few days or more, when he was traveling. It was his typical arrogant attitude that nothing could ever happen to him. That was the attitude I was counting on.

CHAPTER 19

I OPENED THE DOOR and we stepped into the cool patio room that looked out on the pool. Part of the roof was made of glass panels that let the sun in. It was a transition from the main house to the outside and had been a sanctuary for me. Slowly, I led Marty into the main part of the house.

Marty, of course, was drawn to the architecture of the interior. His face was turned up like he was a tourist in New York City. He said, "This is an unbelievable house. Some of the crown work and the fireplace have to be a hundred years old. Done by true craftsmen, too."

I said, "I picked out most of the furniture and the art." As I was standing next to a landscape painted by an up-and-coming Miami artist, I decided to make myself comfortable and slipped over to the wet bar in the corner of the room. I made us a couple of Grey Goose vodkas on the rocks with a splash of cranberry, and we took them back into the patio room, which had loungers and a great view of the pool and yard.

I wanted to prove I wasn't scared, so I stretched out on a

lounger and sipped my drink. Marty followed my lead. The house was so well made, it was difficult to hear anything outside, and I realized that if I was wrong about my calculations, Brennan could show up unannounced at any moment. I wondered what the confrontation would be like. Would it hurt him to see me here with a guy like Marty? Would Marty really try to punch him in the face? These were valid questions, but I was determined not to show any fear.

Brennan had a temper, and I knew there were a few guns in the house. He had bought us a matched set of Walther PPKs one Christmas. He'd made it sound like they were for me, but he really wanted one and pretended I'd appreciate an identical gun for myself. The thought of the guns made me worry about a violent confrontation. Suddenly I started listening for every creak of the house or other sound. We had to be alone.

To fight my fear, I stood up and let Marty look at me for a moment. Before he could ask what I was doing, I slipped out of my shorts and T-shirt and kicked off my flip-flops. Standing there naked, I was waiting for him to tell me I was crazy, but he did the same thing with his bathing suit and tank top.

So there we were, naked, casually sipping drinks inside my former home like we didn't have a care in the world. I tried to imagine what a life like that would be like. A life with Marty instead of the one I'd had with Brennan. It was a nice fantasy.

My doing something like this was all inspired by Marty and his love of dangerous games. This was so outside my comfort zone that Brennan might believe he was seeing things if he walked in right now. I almost wanted to show off the body I'd worked so hard on since he'd given me my walking papers.

I wondered what I might say to the cops if they showed up unexpectedly. Someone might've seen us slipping in from the driveway, or maybe there was a new silent alarm I wasn't aware of. Suddenly, I started thinking of the downside of this adventure that had initially been so exciting. I resisted the urge to jump up and flee. My heart was starting to race, but I kept a pleasant smile on my face as I looked over at Marty, who was examining the room in detail from his comfortable lounger.

Then I heard the mechanical click of a key drift through the house.

Someone was opening the front door.

CHAPTER 20

I FROZE EVERY MUSCLE, naked on the lounger, for just a moment, making sure I hadn't imagined the sound of the key in the dead bolt of the front door. Then I heard the door and I saw the look of panic on Marty's face. What had I done? His games were fun and involved Disney World, and my games were creepy and could lead to jail time.

We both sprang off the loungers and tried to slip into our clothes as quietly as possible. I could hear someone inside the house, and I didn't see how this could turn out short of a disaster.

Marty was dressed faster than me and stood, pulling his shirt tight like he was about to have his photograph taken.

I could hear the footsteps on the marble floor. A steady *click-clack* that could be from hard-soled loafers, the stupid cowboy boots that Brennan occasionally wore, or maybe a policeman's shoes.

We were screwed.

I heard the footsteps more clearly.

Click-clack.

Just as I was about to make a last-ditch effort to lead Marty through the pool house and out into the backyard, where we could be seen through just about every window on the first floor, the French doors to the patio room opened.

We were caught. There was nothing to do but act casual, so I just stood there with the vodka and cranberry in my right hand. I willed myself to turn slowly and then saw the figure in the doorway.

It was not Brennan. The wide waist and short body with flowing dark hair immediately told me it was Alena, Brennan's housekeeper for the past ten years. She'd been here before me and would be here long after me. Most important, she had no beef with me. I'd always treated her well and, frankly, considered having her as a housekeeper as opposed to a younger, shapelier woman a major plus. It was one less thing to tempt Brennan.

Alena gasped when she saw us; then she recognized me. She wore a simple white polyester uniform that stretched tight around her hips and bosom. She held her hands to her cheeks, then rushed toward me with her arms out to envelop me in a massive hug.

"Miss Christy, I have missed you so much. Are you well?" She stepped back and a tear ran down her cheek. "Look at you. You look wonderful. Maybe you could eat a little more, but you are still so beautiful."

That made me shed a tear as I stepped forward and gave Alena my own hug. I'd forgotten how sweet this woman from Guatemala could be. I also knew that not having her phenomenal pastries around was probably one of the reasons I had lost weight quickly after I moved out.

I said, "How are you, Alena?"

She shrugged, and I knew what she meant. She worked for a jerk, but what are you going to do?

I introduced Marty quickly, brushing over our exact relationship.

Alena gave me a sly smile and said, "Very handsome, Miss Christy."

"He's an architect, so I wanted to show him the place. Do you know when Brennan will be back?"

"Not for a long time. He had to go with his father to Miami on business. I was just using the day to run errands."

Now it could get tricky. I hesitated, then finally said, "Alena, do you think you could keep my little visit a secret?"

"I would do anything you asked after the way Mr. Brennan treated you. Besides, now that you're not around, he doesn't even pretend to treat me with any respect. If I didn't need the job so badly, I would walk away and never come back."

I gave Alena another hug before she headed out on her next errand. Now Marty and I had some time to look around.

CHAPTER 21

I DECIDED TO GIVE Marty a grand tour of my former castle. It was a lot like the tours I had given friends and neighbors after we'd had work done around the house. As I was showing him some of the guest bedrooms upstairs and recognizing all the improvements I had made in my years as the mistress of the house, I started to realize that maybe I had been covering up flaws in our marriage by throwing myself so completely into home renovations. It wasn't an uncommon practice among the bored housewives of Palm Beach, but I'd had no idea I was doing it at the time.

I had purposely saved the master bedroom suite for last. It sat on the east side of the second story, and the main windows looked out over the ocean. The view was remarkable. There was a separate walk-in closet on each side of a hallway that led to a bathroom, which included a small steam room, a Roman tub with Jacuzzi jets, Italian marble counters and sinks, and even a massage table that pulled out from one of the marble counters. That saved Brennan's personal masseuse the trouble of carrying a table with her when she stopped by to give him one of his three weekly massages.

I enjoyed the look on Marty's face as he inspected every inch of the house. He said, "This is just unbelievable. Even a spread in *Architectural Digest* wouldn't do this place justice. And most of these renovations were your idea?"

I nodded while trying to hide my superior smile. "That's right, I made this place what it is today. When I got here, Brennan had literally thrown some rugs across the floors and hadn't updated the house in any other way since the 1960s. When I found mold—and I'm talking some serious mold, like up the walls and everything—in two of the guest bedrooms, Brennan's response was 'No one stays there long enough to get sick, so why worry about it?'"

"Peach of a guy. I'm glad I've never had to meet him face-to-face."

"You're in another class. There's no reason for you to ever have to deal with that jackass. He'll be out of our life soon enough."

Marty smiled and said, "Now, that's an attitude I can get behind. As long as you don't need all this again, I can't see why I won't make you happy."

Instead of answering him, I turned and wrapped my arms around his neck, then planted a long, lingering kiss on his lips. It felt nice to have this kind of passion in this particular bedroom. The room certainly hadn't seen this kind of action from me in a long time. I had no idea what Brennan was up to on the dating front, and I didn't care. If I really had to admit it, this house had always meant a lot more to me than Brennan had. At least that was what I kept telling myself.

I pulled Marty by his hand and said, "I have one more thing

I have to show off, and this one will blow your mind." I ignored his questions and pulled him into the walk-in closet, which was really just another room, to the left of the hallway leading to the bathroom. This was Brennan's formal closet, with one entire wall covered by over a hundred suits, organized by cut and color. I knew it would shock Marty.

He was silent for a moment, then whistled as he walked along a row of suits, dragging his finger across the sleeve of each one. He looked up at the dozens of shirts, in colors ranging from white all the way to black, arranged in perfect order. It looked like a paint chart from one end of the closet to the other.

Marty said, "And he wore a different suit every day?"

"Sometimes two; one to work and one to go out at night. The man loves his clothes." I watched Marty poke around the closet; then I said, "Go ahead, take a couple of sports jackets. He'll never notice. Take anything you want. Brennan might be a little taller than you, but you're about the same size. I'm telling you, that asshole will never miss them."

Then I noticed Marty pulling a box from a shelf at the end of the closet and holding it up to show me. It was the box that our matched set of Walther PPK pistols had come in. Brennan's blue steel pistol was still in the box, surrounded by foam padding; an empty space in the shape of a pistol showed where mine used to reside. Now it was safe in the nightstand in my hotel room.

I didn't say anything when Marty pulled the gun from the box and checked to make sure there were cartridges in the magazine. He looked at me for any sign of disapproval, and when I gave none, he slipped the gun into the pocket of his shorts. You couldn't even notice it.

He put the box back right where he'd found it. I knew it would take Brennan months to find out it was empty. Even if he decided to go shooting, he had other guns and might assume he'd stuck the PPK somewhere else. Things like that didn't bother Brennan.

As we slipped out of the house and locked the patio door behind us, I realized I was about to walk down the beach with a man who had just stolen a gun and was carrying it illegally in public in one of the wealthiest cities in America.

This was an exciting game.

CHAPTER 22

MARTY HAD A MANIACAL grin when he turned to me, raised his eyebrows, and said, "This is the big one. You ready for it?" He looked perfect, framed by the rail and the overhang where we were sitting. The sun was just over his head with the Gulfstream Park racetrack behind him.

He held a handful of tickets for the third race and threw in a cartoon madman's laugh. Who wouldn't smile at an act like that? He looked cute, dressed casually in a polo shirt and jeans. This was just another one of his surprises, and I had never been to a horse-racing track before.

Marty knew I loved horses but had been avoiding the polo fields of Wellington because I didn't want to risk running into Brennan. I had casually mentioned it the evening before as we shared a bottle of wine on the beach. That was when he'd come up with this perfect alternative. We'd left this morning for the track in Hallandale Beach. It was a nice ride, about an hour away, and on a weekday, the place wasn't too crowded. The hot dogs were good and the beer was cold. Marty had managed to sweep me off my feet once again.

When the starting gun sounded, the gates opened and the

horses burst out like water from a broken dam. It didn't bother me that there weren't enough people around to make the cheers sound thrilling; I screamed for our horse anyway. We'd put no real thought into making a dozen bets on a horse named Sullivan's Dream. Marty had showed me how to bet on the horse by itself, as well as in combination with other horses, and now we were about to see the result of our leap of faith.

Everything looked good until the third turn, where our horse slowed considerably, and before the race had been decided officially, we realized we were out of the money. Marty said, "Had enough of horses for the day?" He scooped up the losing tickets and stuffed them into his pocket.

"What did you have in mind?" It was warm, and I didn't mind the idea of avoiding Broward County rush hour.

A few minutes later, I found myself on the shuttle heading toward the far reaches of the sprawling parking lot and my white Volvo S-60.

Marty said, "I'll drive, if you don't mind."

I smiled as I thought about what a gentleman he was. Then we slipped onto I-95 and started cruising north.

I said, "This is great. Just what I needed. A few hours away from Palm Beach." I realized that was the opposite of the opinion most people held.

Marty kept his eyes on the road as he said, "Glad you liked it."

"What would you like to do now?"

He thought about it for a few seconds and then said tentatively, "I have a game in mind."

"Anything you want. You've definitely earned it."

Marty just gave me one of his smiles and didn't say anything else. I was content with that. We let Adele's music fill our silence as we zipped along the interstate northbound. I didn't say a word when we passed our exit. Marty had already proved that his surprise trips were always worth the effort.

When we were more than an hour past Palm Beach, I finally said, "Is this all part of your game or are you lost?"

He kept a smile as he said, "All part of the game."

"Want to fill me in?"

He just smiled, and I liked it. He looked a little nervous, with his fingers thumping on the steering wheel and his constant shifting in the seat. I didn't really know what it meant, but I was willing to go along with the game.

We pulled off the interstate and took the long road east until we were on the edges of the city of Vero Beach.

I said, "Okay, I can guess that this game has something to do with your ex-wife. She lives here, right?"

Marty nodded. "She does. You still in?"

"Sure, I said I'll play."

"Then do me a favor and reach back into my jacket on the rear seat."

I twisted and reached for the Windbreaker and immediately felt something heavy in the pocket. I pulled out the pistol and held it up.

"Is this what I think it is?"

Marty grinned and said, "If you think it's the pistol I took from

Brennan's closet." He made it sound innocent, like it was a shoe he had taken.

"What's it for?" I kept my voice as even as possible.

"Our game."

"What's the game?"

"It's called *scare the shit out of my ex-wife, Teal.*" He kept driving, taking a few turns, and said, "Come on, it'll be good for a laugh."

I didn't say yes or no as we parked on a short cul-de-sac a few blocks from the ocean.

Marty pointed at one of the three houses on the right side of the road. A vacant lot took up the space on each side of it, separating it from the houses next door. "That's her house."

It was nice. Nothing like my old house, but it was clean and cute. A short walk to the beach. I was getting nervous as I considered all the crazy things that could happen. But I didn't want to let Marty down, and frankly I was curious as to how he'd scare her. He was a smart guy. I was certain he had put some thought into this.

A brown Audi whipped down the street, then pulled into the driveway.

Marty said, "And heeeeere's Teal." Then he looked at me and said, "Are you sure you want to play? I could really use the help."

I hesitated, then blocked out all the reasons I should say no. Instead I said, "Yeah, I'll play."

CHAPTER 23

MARTY EXPLAINED MY PART of his plan quickly, and I just nodded like a robot. It all sounded crazy to me. All I had to do was distract his ex-wife and he would do the rest. I still had no idea how badly he was going to scare her, but somehow, the idea was enticing. Maybe it was because I wanted to scare Brennan badly that I agreed to go along with everything. This was as close as I could get for now.

We both slipped out of the car, and Marty darted toward a row of bushes that would keep him out of sight. I just started to walk slowly down the street in the direction of Teal's house. I noticed that of the few houses, one of them was empty, with a For Sale sign in the yard, and another house on the corner had no cars in its gravel driveway. On the other side of the street, where we were parked, there were no houses, just the rear of a church soccer field.

Teal was unloading groceries and had to make a couple of trips from the front door to her open trunk.

When I was on the street in front of her house, I got my first good look at Marty's ex-wife. She was a beauty: tall, with a creamy complexion and long, wavy hair. I realized I had never seen a picture of her. I'd done a little snooping on Facebook, but she had no profile.

She noticed me, and I felt my stomach jump. My pulse was racing. I wasn't sure I liked this game.

Teal stared at me for a moment. That pushed me to say, "Hi, I, umm, I'm sorry to bother you, but I just had a stupid flat tire. I was hoping there might be someone who could give me a hand." Marty had said to distract her, but I really hadn't put much thought into it. I hoped this was doing the trick. I figured he'd just slip into the house or do something equally juvenile.

Teal said, "I don't think I'd be much help, but we can call someone. There's a service station less than a mile away."

She didn't sound anything like I'd thought she would. Her voice was warm, and she genuinely seemed interested in helping me. That was a stark contrast to the portrait Marty had painted for me of his ex-wife. She was wearing a simple yellow floral print sundress and looked like a suburban mom who'd brought her kids back home from soccer practice. Suddenly I didn't like the idea of helping Marty scare her.

Teal took a few steps past her open trunk toward me and was just about to say something else when Marty burst out of the bushes and stepped into the yard next to the driveway.

If this was his prank, it worked. Teal jumped and squealed, turning to face her ex-husband. Then she said, "Martin? What the hell are you doing here?"

Right at that point, I realized the game was already spiraling out of control.

CHAPTER 24

NOW THAT MARTY WAS out of the bushes and ready to confront his ex-wife, I didn't see where the real scare was. He didn't have the gun in his hand, and they immediately started to bicker. It was really more awkward than scary, and I have to say I was disappointed by the outcome.

Marty even looked a little confused as Teal started to make her points.

She said, "All you do is complain to me about not being able to pay alimony. How you're so busy you don't have a free minute in the day. But somehow you have time to drive all the way up here from West Palm Beach with your bimbo? That doesn't make any sense, Martin."

Marty just stared at her for a moment, and in all honesty, I felt embarrassed for him. Then he said, "Do you have any idea how you sound? How you are more like a shrieking bird than an actual woman? You've never even met Christy. How dare you call her a bimbo."

"Really, Martin? Really? You're at *my* house, where I moved to get away from your crazy jealousy and stalking, and now you're lecturing me on jumping to conclusions about a woman I've never met?"

Then Teal looked at me. She did not have the scared, confused expression I had been expecting. Instead she said, "Are you part of his plan? You seem bright enough. How did he trick you? Did you just get sucked in slowly to his crazy schemes? It's easy, I know. Everything seems normal until all of a sudden you realize he has no boundaries. His concept of reality is very different than it is for the rest of us. My advice to you would be to run. Just like I did. But apparently I didn't run far enough."

Teal turned back to Marty and said, "Congratulations, Martin, way to impress your new girlfriend. Now, I've got a lot to do, so if you'll excuse me, I need to finish bringing in these groceries."

That felt like a pretty definitive end to our little escapade. I knew Marty wanted the experience to last. He wanted to see fear on her face and maybe expected her to be jealous of me. I'd never really been clear on the goal, but now I could see that coming here had been a mistake. His plan to scare her just hadn't worked out.

Marty reached behind his back, and when his right hand came in front of him he was holding the pistol. I have no idea how badly it scared Teal, but at that moment, I was in absolute shock. I could feel the acid in my stomach back up into my throat. I had never seen a gun pointed at a person before except on TV. I could feel my knees starting to get shaky.

Marty wasn't wearing his normal good-natured smile. He shouted, "You know why I came all the way up here?"

Teal was mesmerized by the gun as she took a step away from Marty. The pretty yellow sundress fluttered in the breeze, but I could see Teal's legs start to shake. Was this the moment Marty had been looking for? Was the terror he was causing his ex-wife enough for him? It was for me.

Teal held both hands out in front of her and said, "I don't know what you're doing, Martin, but this has gone far enough. Put the gun away and we'll forget about this whole stupid encounter."

That sounded good to me. Maybe we hadn't ruined everything. I was about to tell Marty that I wanted to leave when I heard two loud pops. They dissipated in the wide-open space and didn't sound the way I thought gunshots should sound, but the noise, coupled with the bright flashes from the barrel of the gun, told me Marty had snapped.

For a moment, I just held my breath. Time felt like it had stood still. The two of them stood facing each other and hadn't moved a muscle since he'd pulled the trigger. Then Teal slowly turned to face me and I could see two red stains on her pretty yellow floral print dress. One was just below her sternum and the other was along the top of the dress, closer to her right arm.

Teal's mouth moved like she was trying to say something, but no words came out. For a moment I just heard an unsettling bubbling sound; then she kept turning until she fluttered to the hard gravel of the driveway in a heap. Her long hair drifted behind her and settled around her face like a soft blanket.

Slowly I looked at Marty, who was still frozen in place with the gun out in front of him. He looked as if he was as surprised as anyone that the gun had gone off. But he still didn't move. He just stared at the lump of flesh that was his ex-wife, Teal.

Maybe I should've been in shock longer, but immediately the practical part of my brain kicked into gear. I'll admit I had let out a quick scream as soon as Marty fired, but my first real thought was to wonder if anyone had heard the gunshots.

I turned my head, quickly scanned the soccer field behind us, and saw that there was no one outside the church. There were those vacant lots on each side of Teal's house, and when I looked up the street I saw nothing but one car passing on US 1. I didn't think the sound of the shots would've carried very far. They'd happened so close together that it would be difficult for someone to pinpoint where they had come from.

Taking everything in and making a quick assessment led me to yell at Marty, "We need to go, right now!"

God forgive me, but it wasn't until we were in my car and Marty was driving south on US 1 that I even thought about whether we should have checked Teal to see if she was still alive.

CHAPTER 25

"HOLY SHIT, WHAT HAVE I done? Holy shit, what have I done?" Marty kept chanting that same phrase like it was some kind of mantra that would bring him back to reality. Or maybe it would *keep* him from reality. Because at this moment, as we tried to gain some perspective and figure out what we would do next, we knew that we were both involved in a murder.

My car swerved as Marty overreacted to a car pulling up to a side street.

I screamed, "What the hell are you doing? We need to draw *less* attention to ourselves, not more!" I immediately regretted being so sharp. I was on edge, and looking at Marty, who was perspiring uncontrollably and leaning into the steering wheel, I knew he was, too.

He took the turn onto Kings Highway, and I knew we'd be cutting through some odd little neighborhoods just north of Fort Pierce.

"Where are you going?" I asked with the stress still evident in my voice.

"The turnpike."

"Listen, Marty, we have to take a deep breath and think this through. You want to go to a road that will photograph us entering and ping off my SunPass as we pay the toll? We need to stay on the back roads, or at most, get on I-95."

I could see that my words were registering with him. He said, "Do you think anyone saw us? It just sort of happened. I didn't even know what I was doing."

I felt like I was about to throw up. I'd never been involved in anything at all like this. I had talked to the cops more in the last couple of weeks than I had in my whole life combined. If I'd been counting on Marty being my rock, I could see I'd made a mistake. Even if I went to the police right now, I'd have to explain why I'd driven all the way up to Vero Beach with Marty and why we'd both fled the scene. This wouldn't play out well in any courtroom. Now we had to jump in with both feet.

Marty turned onto one of the main roads and then took the entrance ramp to I-95. I didn't want to question his every move; he was already so far over the edge that I even wondered if he might pull the gun and use it on himself or maybe even on me. If we got stopped by a cop now, it would all be over. There was no way he'd be able to look calm with the way he was acting.

"Speed up and get into the center lane. You're drawing attention," I snapped when I looked at the speedometer and saw that he was only going forty-eight miles an hour. Cars whizzed past us like we were parked.

Marty mumbled something as he got into the flow of traffic. He was still staring straight ahead, and I tried to figure out how to get the gun from him. That would be a good first step. Eliminate the possibility of more murders or a suicide.

I leaned over and patted him on the shoulder and rubbed his neck for a minute. He didn't respond. The guy was a wreck. Then I let my hand drift down between the seat and his back until I felt the grip of the pistol tucked into his belt on the right side of his back.

I didn't say anything; I just pulled out the small semiautomatic pistol and slipped it into the console.

Marty saw where I put the gun but didn't say anything. I felt like I might have relieved some of the pressure he was feeling by taking the gun from him.

I said, "Marty, we're going to have to come up with a decent alibi to get through this."

"I know, I know. I still can't believe what just happened."

"The last place anyone can prove we visited was Gulfstream Park. I think I have one of the betting slips in my purse."

"I have a whole bunch crammed in my pocket."

"Good, good. We just say we stayed at the park until later in the afternoon, then took I-95 back to Palm Beach. We'll make sure someone sees us as soon as we get into town. We can go to the Palm Beach Grill and have a drink. If we hurry, we can be there by five thirty and it will match up with leaving the racetrack about four." I waited for some kind of response from my semicomatose boyfriend. Then I said, "We're going to have a drink and gather ourselves. We won't mingle with anyone unless we have to, but we at least want the bartenders to see us."

He took his eyes off the road and stared at me for a moment but didn't say anything. I had to gasp and point at the slow Mazda in front of us to get him to look back at the highway and swerve into the right lane.

"Trust me, babe, this is the only thing we can do."

He took the exit at Jupiter before I could say anything. He said, "I don't know why, but I feel like it's a better idea to drive down to US 1 here and then south to Palm Beach. Maybe it's an instinct. Does that sound right to you?"

Suddenly he sounded coherent and in control. "Yeah, that sounds good, Marty. Just keep cool and it'll all work out. But there's one other thing we need to talk about."

"What's that?"

"No matter what happens, you know the police are going to talk to you, if for no other reason than the fact that you're Teal's ex-husband. You have to face them and be cool and composed during the whole meeting. They might come as soon as tonight. They'll try to trip you up on details. You have to be careful with what you say."

"Talk to me about what? We've been at the track all day, then stopped for a drink at the Palm Beach Grill. I can account for almost every minute of my day."

"And I'll back you up on every single thing you say. But we need to practice our story over and over. And not be on the phone to each other every few minutes."

He nodded. "Smart, very smart. I'm lucky I have you." He focused on the street in front of him, careful not to cause an accident or draw any attention. If someone spotted us up here at the north end of the county, it would blow all our plans instantly.

I leaned back in the seat and took a deep breath. I tried to clear my mind, but all I could see was that dark blood spreading across Teal's pretty flowered dress. I was an accomplice to murder.

CHAPTER 26

ABOUT MIDDAY, I TURNED on my phone and called Marty. We didn't want a lot of phone calls that could be verified by the police. We felt it would be more natural if we had just one call during the day like any normal couple. That was all part of the plan we'd formulated on our frantic drive down from Vero Beach when we decided to try to cover up our involvement in the murder of his ex-wife. Once we'd made a conscious decision to hide it, we were committed.

We met at TooJay's, a decent local deli chain that was in the same plaza as the Palm Beach Grill. It was later in the afternoon, so the place was nearly empty except for a few of the elderly residents who'd walked over from the Biltmore Condos and a couple of traders from the local financial companies grabbing a late, late lunch.

We picked at a platter because neither of us felt much like eating, and when we were sure no one was around, Marty said, "So the cops came by my apartment late last night. It was a Vero detective and an agent from the Florida Department of Law Enforcement. I guess they needed the FDLE for jurisdiction. They didn't call first. Just knocked on my door around eleven. I acted like they woke me up, but of course I couldn't sleep."

This was what I had been anxious to hear all night. I couldn't believe I'd managed to keep my cool. I'd wanted to race over to see him or call him the entire day. "What'd you tell them?"

Marty leaned in close and said, "Just like we practiced. We went to the racetrack, then drove almost straight home to the Palm Beach Grill. I dropped you off at the Brazilian Court about nine. I hadn't heard from or talked to Teal in a couple of months. I even left my betting slips in the front pocket of my jeans so I had them when the cops asked if I had any proof I'd been at the track. It worked out exactly like you said it would."

I said, "They came by to see me about noon. Maybe they were checking some other details about your story first."

"What'd you tell them?"

"Same thing. Just like we practiced. Not too much detail. The difference is *I* really was asleep when they knocked on the door."

We sat for a few minutes, nibbling corned beef and turkey off the platter. Then Marty said, "I'm still in shock over what happened. It was like I wasn't even there. I have no idea what came over me. I hope you can see that wasn't the real me yesterday. I want you to know I'm a good man."

I took the opening to a question I needed to ask. "Teal said you drove her to move. What did she mean?"

Marty shrugged. "Nothing. She said I couldn't let it go, but I could. She overreacted and got a restraining order during our divorce proceedings. The judge seemed like he was only listening to her and didn't care about my side of the story at all. But the restraining order was just to make her look like a victim. It was a horrible experience that got me really down on myself. But once I met you, it was a lot easier."

I said, "You saved all those betting slips and asked me to use my Volvo. I have to ask: Was shooting Teal part of a spur-of-the-moment game or did you plan it?"

He gave me a puppy-dog look and said, "I'd never put you in that position. It just happened. I was just as shocked as you were that it happened, but now I think it might all work out. I think if they had enough, the cops would've arrested me. We're in the clear, and I feel like this is all going to be okay."

I said, "I hope so, because…"

"What? Come on, you can tell me."

"Marty, I love you. Sometimes it takes stress or danger to reveal exactly how you feel about someone. I love you, and I would do anything for you."

He looked relieved. Finally he said, "I've been wanting to tell you how I feel for a long time, but I was afraid I might scare you off. I mean with your divorce and all, I didn't want to add anything to your plate. I love you, too." He reached across the table and lifted my hand so he could kiss it.

I couldn't keep from glancing around the nearly empty restaurant and wondering if any of the patrons could be cops.

CHAPTER 27

IT WAS DARK BY the time we left TooJay's, and we decided to just walk around to the other side of the plaza and stop into the Palm Beach Grill for a few drinks. God knew we could use some alcohol.

We sat at the same high-top as the night we met. The waitress, Suzie, a cute little thing I'd known since she started here, gave us an odd look. A minute later she was back with two Grey Goose vodkas with cranberry. Both doubles. Marty threw his down quickly and looked at Suzie and said, "May I have another, please." Then he stood up and said, "I have to go to the bathroom."

As soon as he was away from the table, Suzie looked at me and said, "The cops were here right when we opened. They asked about you and Marty. They asked if we saw you in here often and if you were here last night. Is everything okay?"

"Just a misunderstanding."

"But you're sure you're okay? I mean, there's nothing funny going on with Marty?"

I let out a laugh. "No, he's not holding me hostage or anything. He is a little stressed out, so if you don't mind making his drinks a little stronger so he can relax, I'd appreciate it. We're going to have a serious talk."

Suzie was a good waitress and kept the drinks coming without either of us having to ask. After a while, Marty and I shared a hamburger and nibbled at the fries. Marty had walked over to say hello to one of his clients from the island who was putting in a separate pool for his children and wanted a new patio with two enclosed rooms built around it.

There was a TV on in the corner, and I saw a local news piece on Teal's murder. Vero Beach was on the very edge of the local news territory, and the story had gained some interest because shootings generally didn't occur in an upscale town like that.

I stared at the TV, relieved Marty wasn't at the table to see it. The pretty, young female reporter spoke in front of Teal's cute house, and the story was interspersed with footage and earlier interviews. One of them was with a police detective who said absolutely nothing about the facts of the case other than to give the information that they had a body and no witnesses. A photo of Teal flashed on the screen. She was dressed up like she was going to a fancy party or a ball. It suddenly struck me as sad.

The reporter said, "Anyone with any information about this horrendous crime can call Crime Stoppers or the Vero Beach Police Department." It made me think about what had happened and how Marty had snapped so unexpectedly.

The news story headed for its conclusion with the reporter saying, "Police are working around the clock to solve the murder of Teal Hawking. Evidence is still being analyzed, and interviews are being conducted." Then the story ended with the police detective declaring, "We won't stop until this case is solved."

Marty walked back to the table as I processed that last remark. We sat, silently watching all the rich and wannabe-rich people as they came and went through the restaurant's door. After Marty had downed a double vodka, I finally said, "You feel like another game?" His eyes were a little woozy, but he was still in control.

"Sure. What'd you have in mind?"

"A good game of make-believe."

CHAPTER 28

MARTY JUST STARED AT me. "A game of make-believe?"

"It's only fair. You owe me this one."

Marty leaned back and raised his hands. "I'm not arguing. Anything you want."

I said, "Anything?"

"Anything at all." That smile said he was sincere.

I let him consider his words and just gazed into his eyes. He really was a good-looking man and a lot of fun to hang out with. I said, "Let's go see Brennan. I need a little confrontation with him. I want to settle our differences, and he needs to see I've moved on. I want the satisfaction of him seeing us as a couple. Then I'm going to tell him you make me feel like he never could."

"What do I have to do?"

I smiled and patted his hand as I said, "Just look pretty."

"I can do that." He gave me a sly smile and said, "I can do a lot more if you want. I'd like to see that prick piss his pants."

I thought about it, imagining Brennan with urine staining his expensive slacks, and it made me smile. Marty tended to make me smile.

"I just feel like there's something I have to get off my chest with that guy."

"Are you kidding? Brennan treated you terribly, and you have a right to get anything you want off your chest. He needs a dose of his own medicine."

"I couldn't agree more."

When Marty wandered off again, I grabbed four twenties from my purse and laid them on the table. I wanted to scoot out of there with minimum fuss.

My friend Lisa Martz, who had introduced Marty and me, came through the front door and saw me. She came right to the table and gave me a hug.

Lisa said, "Look at you, aren't you a vision. How's it going with Marty?"

Before I could answer, Marty was next to her, ready with a hug.

I didn't feel like chatting. I was focused. I wanted to have it out with Brennan. I felt my impatience grow as Lisa chatted about the most Palm Beach of things: houses, cars, and scandals.

When Lisa moved on to another table to spread the gossip of the island, Marty and I were alone. He said, "When do you want to play this little game of yours?"

"Why not tonight?"

CHAPTER 29

I HAD TO STOP at the Brazilian Court and left Marty in the car. I stopped and spoke with Allie at the front desk, then rushed to my room. One advantage of living in such a tiny space is that nothing ever takes long to find. I was back in the car in a few minutes and found Marty listening to the Moody Blues on the radio.

As I drove through Palm Beach with Marty in the passenger seat, he surprised me by showing some nerves. It wasn't about a confrontation, either.

Marty said, "Do I look all right to meet Brennan?"

I laughed and said, "You're not going to date him. You look fine."

"I mean, will I impress him the way you want me to?" He blew into his hand and smelled his breath. "God, I need a mint at least." He dug in the glove compartment, then turned to the console. That was where he found the pistol I'd stuck in there the day before.

He reached down, pulled out the gun, and examined it for a second, then said, "We'll take this, too. I hate to admit it, but somehow it makes me feel more confident."

If Marty was hesitant to play this game, it didn't show as he slipped the gun into his pants and pulled his shirt out over it.

By the time we were in front of my old house, Marty was looking around to make sure no one was on the street. This was Palm Beach and it was after nine o'clock, so that wasn't even a worry.

Both the Bentley and the Jaguar were in the driveway, and I could see the downstairs den lights on. That meant Brennan was home. He was the only one who used the den; he'd sit in there when he was working late to keep up with the foreign stock exchanges. We sat in the car and watched the house for a few minutes. Then I saw Brennan's silhouette as he stood up from the desk and walked to one of the file cabinets that were built into the wall.

There was no traffic this time of night, but I kept twisting my head from side to side just to make sure. I was nervous, and there was no hiding it. Not only was my heart still pounding, but I felt a thin sheen of sweat across my forehead. Maybe this wasn't such a good idea.

I turned to Marty and said, "Okay, when we get out, don't slam the door, just close it quietly." He nodded obediently.

I said, "You sure you're still up for this, babe?"

"Anything for you."

"Brennan can be a lot to deal with. For all his bluster, he does have a mean streak, and he's not afraid to show it."

"I can handle myself." Marty sounded confident.

"I just want to say what I have to say and get out of here. Okay?"

"Okay, okay. I'll behave."

I looked up at my grand house and thought about how much my life had changed in the past six months. It made me angry.

Before I had time to dwell on my emotions, a splash of light fell across us. A car had just turned and was coming down the street slowly. We were parked awkwardly on the curb where there wasn't supposed to be any parking. We stuck out like a sore thumb. Then I realized that at this time of night, it was likely a police car on patrol. I didn't feel like answering questions in front of my estranged husband's house.

Then I thought of the real problem. What if they pulled us out of the car and found the gun on Marty? That would not go over well here in Palm Beach.

I looked at Marty and saw the same concerns on his face.

We both stared at the car as it came toward us at a steady pace like a shark moving methodically through the water. Neither of us could find the will to move.

Marty was about to say something when I held up my hand to keep him quiet. I needed to think.

Then, as the car was almost on top of us, I noticed it was a bright red. Not the blue and white of a Palm Beach police car. And it was a Cadillac. A big one. As the car passed us, I could see the tiny white head that barely reached over the dash, and I realized it was a local, someone who probably always drove slowly after dark.

The elderly woman never even looked in our direction.

I let out a long breath and grabbed my purse from the backseat, and we slipped out of the car.

CHAPTER 30

WE MADE IT UP the driveway to the front door without making a sound. For some reason, when we stood in front of the door I found myself out of breath. I pressed the doorbell and could hear the chimes inside the house. Chimes I'd picked out and had installed to replace the stupid *ding-dong* sound that was attached to the doorbell when we got married. I looked around, making sure no one was watching us. Marty tapped his foot as he stood next to me.

It was a typical humid Florida night, and the breeze off the Atlantic felt like heaven. The excitement of facing Brennan built inside me. I turned to Marty, and in a low voice I said, "I can't wait to see the look on Brennan's face."

Then the door opened, and Brennan didn't disappoint me. He was utterly shocked and couldn't hide it. Dressed in a polo shirt and golf slacks, he looked good. Almost like a model. His hair was perfect, and he had a few lines on his face, like a man who spent much of his time outdoors. For a change, he was speechless, and his blue eyes were wide with surprise. He looked from me to

Marty slowly, then settled back on me. This was exactly what I wanted. He was shaken.

After a long silence, Brennan said, "Christy, what are you doing here at this hour? I thought we were speaking only through our attorneys."

I took a moment to gather myself, looking Brennan straight in the eyes as I said, "I need to say something. Not in court, where I can be censored."

"I'm listening," he said slowly, still looking back and forth between me and Marty.

Somehow with just those two words he managed to be condescending.

"Do you realize what a pretentious, pompous ass you are? Is it intentional?"

Brennan made no comment.

"You're rich, so what? You've never had any hardships, so basically you're spoiled, and I enabled you for four years. You didn't need a wife, you needed a caretaker. I didn't complain when you left me at home alone on Christmas two years in a row so you could windsurf with your buddies in Aruba. You basically ignored my parents and to this day don't know my mom's first name. And you had no reason to try in our marriage, so you just threw me out like the trash. I've got news for you, Brennan. I'm not who you thought I was." I took a breath, then said, "I gave you four years and you gave me nothing in return."

"Except a phenomenal lifestyle."

"And the privilege of being Mrs. Brennan Moore."

"Glad you finally get it."

That arrogant smile cut into my soul.

I kept going. "You spent more on a massage table built into the bathroom than on my engagement ring. That should've given me an idea of what to expect when I married you. You told the judge you didn't think I had ever shown any real emotion toward you. Well, be careful what you wish for. Now you'll see all my emotions at once. All my well-earned anger and frustration, followed by relief and joy. Now you get to know what it feels like to be powerless."

I think Marty could sense my anger, but he shocked me when, without any warning, he yanked the pistol from under his shirt, fumbled with it for a second, and then pointed it at Brennan's groin. He held it steady in his hand as he brought his face up to look at my reaction.

I was at a loss. He'd moved so quickly I hadn't expected it.

Marty was smiling.

Brennan staggered back half a step and said, "Jesus Christ, that's my gun."

CHAPTER 31

I FELT LIKE SINGING. Why not? I was back inside my house. For the moment I could forget the awkward fact that Marty was holding a gun on Brennan. We shuffled in through the foyer, then turned into Brennan's den, where it was clear he'd been working. His computer screen was still showing active trades on the foreign stock exchanges, and he had papers laid out across his giant oak desk. The one I had found for him in a furniture shop in North Carolina. It was magnificent, with hardwood inlays and drawers that felt like they moved on air.

Brennan had been remarkably quiet up to this point, but he still had that self-assured, superior look on his face, even with Marty standing a few feet away pointing the gun at him. It was clear Brennan didn't think we were going to hurt him. Obviously, we'd been drinking, and I'm sure Brennan just viewed it as another immature prank by a dull wife he thought he'd gotten rid of. But after a minute or so, he was tired of the game and anxious to get back to work.

He had his hands up slightly, like he was being robbed. It must have been human instinct. He kept his voice low as he said, "Could you point that somewhere else, please."

Marty just said, "Nope."

It was the best possible response to unnerve Brennan. It also shut him up. He stared at Marty but wisely remained silent.

Marty cut his eyes to me in an effort to get a clear idea of what we had planned. He was visibly more agitated than when we'd started this little prank and was hopping from one foot to the other like a nervous kid who needed to go to the bathroom. He was probably wondering if I expected him to gun down Brennan like he had Teal the day before. I stepped over to him, patted him on the back, gently wrapped my hand around the gun, and eased it from his tight grip, quietly saying, "It's going to be okay." He visibly relaxed as he relinquished the pistol and took a pace backward.

Now I held the gun. I took a breath to calm down. Marty was about to snap, and I was sure I'd taken the pistol just in time. As I stepped away from him, closer to Brennan, I told Marty, "Just wait right there, sweetheart, and keep calm."

Brennan picked up on the fact that I was trying to keep Marty from doing anything crazy, and he thought we were looking for a way out. He waited while I made sure the pistol was pointed down, away from anyone's vital organs.

Marty appeared a little hurt that I had taken the gun from him. If I had acted a little faster the day before, maybe poor Teal would still have been alive. The gun was heavy in my hand. Heavier than I remembered it from the range. I carefully slipped it into the pocket of my jeans. It fit snugly.

Brennan was visibly relieved and regained some of his swagger. He raised his voice and said, "You found some moron you can order around and you think it's love? Christy, what in the hell are you guys doing here? This doesn't help anyone. You guys need to get out of my house and sober up."

That's when I straightened up and looked him right in the eye and said, "I'm not drunk. In fact, I've barely had a drink all night." I realized that surprised Marty, too, as he looked at me with a puzzled expression.

Then I reached into my purse, the one large purse I owned, and easily drew out another pistol. The second one of the matched set. It looked identical and rendered both men absolutely mute. I liked that.

I gave my full attention to Marty. "I'm afraid there's a lot you don't understand, sweetheart. And I don't think you'll ever realize how much this bothers me." He still had that look like a puppy as I stepped closer to Brennan, standing just behind him and facing Marty. "I mean it, Marty, I am really, really sorry." Then I aimed the pistol and squeezed the trigger. Just like I had been taught. By Brennan. The pistol bucked in my hand and the noise inside the house, with all the marble and tile, sounded like a nuclear blast.

But I still managed to hit my target and shot Marty once, almost dead center in his chest.

The flash from the muzzle blinded me temporarily. I didn't even see any bloodstain on his shirt before he dropped straight to the floor, and thankfully, he didn't make any sounds like Teal had. He rolled onto his back, and then everything stopped. He was absolutely still. My ears rang from the gunshot, and the air had the acrid odor of gunpowder. Marty was dead. It had been quick, and he was now flat on a hard wooden floor that would be easy to clean up.

I'd noticed how much Brennan had jumped when I pulled the trigger. I couldn't see his face, but I could imagine what he was thinking right now. His legs were already trembling.

Good God, this was what I had been waiting for.

CHAPTER 32

I WAS STILL STANDING behind Brennan, who dared not turn his head. He had a perfect view of Marty's crumpled body about fifteen feet in front of him. My ears still throbbed from the noise of the gunshot. Now I knew why we always wore earplugs when we went to the range. My guess was that right about now, Brennan was regretting our days shooting together and his detailed lessons. At the time, he'd just enjoyed being able to tell me things. It had been a power trip for him.

Brennan's voice cracked as he said, "Christy, Jesus Christ, what have you done?" He choked up on whatever he was going to say next as he tried not to vomit.

"How's it feel, Brennan? Knowing you're helpless. Is it a new sensation?" I let a brief silence fall over the room so I could enjoy seeing Brennan squirm. Now he was shaking as he tried to maintain his composure. The air was still filled with the odor of the gunshot. This old house had never seen anything like this, and Brennan had never experienced anything like it either. He deserved it. Not just for the way he'd treated me, but for the way he treated the rest of the world. It was time he learned he wasn't better than anyone else.

I said, "I doubt the sound of the shot even penetrated the walls. No one outside this room has any idea what just happened. No one is coming to help." I let that sink in, then said, "Stand there perfectly still, looking straight ahead. Got it?"

He nodded frantically. Sweat stains were now visible on the back of his shirt near his underarms. I don't think I'd ever seen Brennan sweat.

I said, "I'd like to savor your reaction to this, but I have a lot to do."

"What—what are you talking about? What do you have to do?" He started to whimper and added, "What's going on? I don't understand what you're doing."

"I think experts call it 'arranging the crime scene.'" I stayed behind him as I snapped on a pair of gloves. I'd figured out the right trajectories and what the residue tests would show. "You see, Brennan, it took a lot of research to learn that the cops might connect the gun to Teal's murder. I had to take all that into account and come up with the right story."

"Story? What story? You're going to try to make the police believe *I* shot your boyfriend?"

I chuckled. "I have no doubt I could sell any story to the cops at this point. It's all the other details that take concentration." There was a long silence as Brennan thought things over.

He finally said with a cry, "What are you doing? I don't understand."

"Well, Brennan, dear. This was my backup plan. I admit I had another one in the works for quite some time, almost from the day I met Marty, who I recognized as being very nice and extremely easy to manipulate. I knew if my legal challenges to your ridiculous prenuptial agreement failed, I'd need an alternative. This is it.

"I knew I wanted to go through with the plan the day you crushed me in court just because you could." I let him think about that and how he had abused me. "Yesterday, Marty shot his ex-wife. You might've seen it on the news. He got away with it, too. At least he thought he'd gotten away with it. I told him I had backed up his alibi"—I leaned in close to Brennan and whispered in his ear—"but I didn't."

Now I pulled the gun from my pocket and held it in my right hand. The other was loose in my left, hanging by my side. I slowly strolled around in front of Brennan until I was standing near Marty's body. "Marty was crazy for Teal and everyone knew it. She even got a restraining order on him. I told the cops we left the racetrack early and I didn't know where Marty was most of the afternoon until I met him at the Palm Beach Grill." Now I could enjoy Brennan's expression as I laid out my story.

"That's why I'll say I broke up with him earlier tonight at the Palm Beach Grill and why I told my friend Allie, at the Brazilian Court, that I had already broken up with him and I was a little scared. I also told her Marty went crazy when he heard you were interested in reconciling with me. It's also why I'm sure the police are at Marty's apartment waiting for him right now."

I held the gun steady in front of me. "The best part, the one thing that just fell into place, was when Marty found your pistol. I may have moved it so he'd notice it, but he thought it was all his idea." I saw that Brennan was confused. "That's right, he found it in your closet one day when we came to visit. I didn't say a word when he stole the pistol. Because I knew the cops could tie the gun that killed Teal to the gun used here tonight, I had to switch them on poor, simple Marty. Wild, huh? He used *my* gun to shoot Teal and I used *your* gun to shoot him. All I have to say is that Marty stole my gun from the nightstand in my hotel room. It will work out perfectly. Brilliant, right?"

Brennan was trying to keep from sobbing. "What are you talking about? Why are you doing this?"

I grinned. "Because I can. And there's not a damn thing you can do about it."

CHAPTER 33

I COULDN'T BELIEVE HOW thrilling it was to have this much power over another person. It almost made me understand why Brennan had done some of the things he had. Now it was time to explain exactly what was about to happen as I stood in front of him, holding the gun in a remarkably steady hand.

"It's really a simple story. The key is to always keep things simple. Marty asked to go for one final drive together. Then he pulled the gun, the Walther PPK you gave me as a present. He must've gotten it out of my nightstand at the hotel. Then he forced me to drive here so he could prove he loved me, because he was, you know, crazy.

"He came into the house and you shot each other. I was terrified and fled upstairs to call 911. Simple and believable."

Brennan just stared at me. "But why? This could ruin your whole life. What do you really have to gain?"

I let out a quick laugh. I'd never realized Brennan could be so funny. Then I looked at him with a deadpan stare and said, "You have no will. I checked the wall safe the other day when we were here. And I know you're far too cocky to leave it with an attorney."

Brennan had a real hitch in his voice now. "So what? We're divorced. What good does all this do you?"

"Actually, we're in the *process* of divorcing. We might even reconcile. If you die intestate—that means with no will—I get my house back. It's really all I wanted. I couldn't care less if you live or die. And frankly, I would've preferred a nice fella like Marty to live with. But shit happens."

"I can make this right, I swear. You can have the house. You can have a great settlement. You name it."

"It's a little late to negotiate, Brennan. You had your chance to do this the right way. Now I've just turned it into a big game. A game of make-believe. Let's make believe we're part of a fantastic murder mystery. Now you have to make believe you're going to die."

I let that realization dawn on him so I could see it in his face. It was amazing. One moment he thought I was ranting and raving, and the next he realized I was following through on a carefully laid-out plan.

I said, "Every game has a winner and a loser. I'm afraid in this one you're the loser, babe." I squeezed the trigger and the gun jumped in my hand. The bullet flew a little high, hitting Brennan in the upper chest. He toppled backward and fell with a thud on the hard floor, gurgling for a few seconds. This time the noise didn't shock me so much and the gunpowder smell wasn't as jolting. Everything is easier the second time around. Even shooting a man.

It took only a minute to wipe down the guns and stick one in the right hand of each of the dead men in the room. I pulled the trigger with the gun in the hand of each man and didn't really care where the bullet went. It was all part of the story I had planned.

I stepped back to make sure everything looked just the way I wanted it to. The bodies were well separated, and the police measurements would show that the bullets had traveled about the right distance. I went to the nearest bathroom and, using the back of my hand to avoid leaving fingerprints, double-flushed the gloves. Perfect.

I strolled through the house and started to climb the stairs, then dialed 911 on my cell phone, and as soon as the operator answered, I screamed, "They're shooting each other, they're shooting each other, what should I do?" Then I threw in a convincing cry.

The operator, keeping calm like they're trained to, said, "Ma'am, ma'am, where are you? What's the address?"

I continued to climb the stairs. Through a series of sobs I gave her the address. And told her, "He's crazy and he has a gun."

The operator said, "Where are you in the house? Are you safe?"

I gave her a good moan and said, "I'm hiding upstairs in a closet. Think I'm safe for now."

The operator said, "Stay there. Help is on the way."

When the cops found me in the closet, they would see that I'd been crying. What they wouldn't understand was that they were tears of joy. I had just gotten my house back by winning a game. This game was called *let's play make-believe that I can get away with the murder of my husband.*

On the day of the opening ceremony of the Olympic Games, an athlete goes missing...

Read on for an extract

FOR THIRTY-NINE LONG YEARS, the telephone on Juliana's side of the bed has rung out in the middle of the night, the same way it is ringing right now. Juliana has never complained. Not one time. Whenever it happens, she just hands me the receiver, and tells me not to get myself killed.

The phone is on Juliana's side of the bed because there is nothing on my side except a wall. I earn a cop's wages, and we live in a house the size of a shoebox. I roll over and press the tiny button on my black plastic Casio and it lights up. 4 a.m.

'Carvalho?' Vitoria Paz, my partner for the past two years, is the voice on the end of the line.

I grunt. My bones hurt.

'I hate to wake you.'

'Everyone hates to wake me,' I tell her. 'That's why they always wake you first.'

I hear her sigh, but I know she's smiling.

'I'll be at your place in five minutes.'

She's talking out of the side of her mouth because she's smoking. She smokes a lot. Paz is twenty-six years old and tough as nails.

'What's the deal?' I ask, rolling out of bed.

'Missing person.'

I pull on socks in the dark. I'm an expert at this.

'Won't they still be missing after I've had a decent night's sleep?'

I hear Paz take another drag on her cigarette.

'The missing guy is an athlete,' she says. 'So you know how that goes at the moment.'

I know exactly how that goes. The Olympic Games officially open in a few hours' time, and the world's media are in Rio. Actually, the whole world is in Rio. And everyone, from the President down, is nervous.

'How long has this athlete been gone?'

'Twelve hours,' Paz says. 'Get some coffee down your neck – you sound irritable.'

I put the phone back on the beaten-up dresser as quietly as I can, but I hear Juliana stir.

'Rafael,' she says. 'Don't get yourself killed.'

I promise her that I won't, and I listen to her breathing soften. As Juliana slips back into her dreams, I use the blue backlight of the Casio to guide me out of the bedroom and down into the kitchen. I set the kettle on the stove and pull my badge and gun from the cupboard above the refrigerator. Soon Paz's headlights wash through the kitchen window and I get a first glimpse of myself in the mirror. I look crumpled. My hair is longer than it should be; still mostly brown, but greying at the temples. I haven't shaved for two days and I'm wearing yesterday's shirt. It's fair to say I've looked better.

Behind the wheel of her tiny Fiat, Paz looks fresh. The car reeks of smoke as I get in. It's warm out, and Paz is wearing a tight black vest and jeans. Paz runs three times a week, boxes at a local gym and benches one hundred and forty pounds. She hides her strength and grit behind a perfect white smile, sparkling brown eyes and a mop of black hair, which frames her face in tight spirals.

'Morning, Carvalho.'

'Morning. You okay?'

'Better than you, by the looks of things.'

I smile.

'That's not saying so much.'

Paz pulls slowly off the drive and doesn't hit the accelerator properly until we're out of earshot of Juliana. Paz swears like a bartender and smokes like a chimney, but whenever she is around my wife, she acts like an altar girl on her way to church. Soon enough, though, she puts her foot to the floor and I'm holding onto my scalding coffee with calloused fingers, hoping to Christ that she doesn't hit a pothole and scar me for life.

'Do you have to drive quite so fast? I'm two weeks off retirement and I'd like to get there alive, if it's all the same to you. It's a missing-person case, not a shootout.'

Paz smiles. She loves it when I'm grouchy. She has one hand on the wheel and is using the other to cram a new cigarette into her mouth, before flicking a steel Zippo to light it.

'The missing athlete is Tim Gilmore,' she says. 'Have you heard of him?'

'The Australian guy?'

I have an image of Tim Gilmore in my head. He's Australia's poster boy, and I've seen the pictures of him on billboards and adverts around the city. He's blond, tanned and tall.

'Javelin, right?'

Paz nods as the cigarette catches. Her eyes narrow against the smoke, making her look like a Mexican bandit scanning the horizon for trouble.

'Yeah. He's their team captain, too,' Paz says, taking another drag. 'Twenty-seven years old. It's his second Olympics. He's got a strong chance of a medal. At least he would, if anybody knew where he was.'

We pass rows of houses as the tiny Fiat speeds across the city. My free hand, the one that isn't holding the coffee, is holding onto the edge of the seat. The fabric has worn through over the years and exposed the foam underneath. There's a hole where Paz's five-year-old boy Felipe has been picking away at it with his tiny fingers. He's the only person who sits in Paz's passenger seat more often than me. Each time I get into her car, the hole in the foam is bigger.

'Felipe's like a moth in a wardrobe,' I tell her. 'This seat's going to disappear eventually.'

Paz doesn't bite.

'Gilmore trained late yesterday afternoon,' she says. 'But he never showed up to eat with his team in the evening. He's not answering his phone, either.'

'Late afternoon?' I push the blue backlight on my watch. 'That's only twelve hours ago.'

'I know,' Paz says as she winds down the window and flicks out her cigarette butt. 'Makes you wonder why they're so twitchy, doesn't it?'

'Get used to it,' I tell her. 'It's gonna be like the World Cup all over again. Everybody is going to be watching their backs and covering their behinds for the next two weeks, and if anything goes wrong they'll go ballistic.'

Suddenly Paz slams on the brakes and we come to a stop with a tyre screech loud enough to wake a city block. I look at her sideways as I swill down the last of my coffee and put the cup on the dashboard.

'Was that really necessary?'

'Nope,' she grins. 'But it felt good. Anyway, we're here.'

We park up on Rua Carioca, surrounded by thirty-one high-rise blocks full of the world's most talented athletes. Nearly four thousand flats. New coffee shops, flower shops and post offices have sprung up on every corner. But right now, everything is closed and deserted.

'Party central,' Paz says. 'Not.'

She is right. The air is still and the lights behind the thousands of windows are almost all turned off.

'Athletes love to sleep. It's one of the few things I have in common with them these days. Come on.'

Gilmore's coach is waiting for us in the lobby.

'Hunter Brown,' he says in a broad Aussie accent. He has a firm, dry handshake and bright, attentive eyes, just the right side of furtive.

'Carvalho,' I say. 'And this is Detective Paz.'

Vitoria shakes his hand.

'Has he shown up yet?'

Brown shakes his head. I frown as we walk over to a couple of sofas at the far side of the lobby. Hunter Brown looks away, composing his thoughts.

'I get it,' he says. 'You probably think I'm overreacting.'

I say nothing.

'Listen. Tim has trained for four years for this event. He wouldn't run out on us now. Not unless something is very wrong.'

He's genuinely worried.

'Has he ever gone missing before?' Paz asks.

Brown shakes his head.

'No way. We've been locked on this schedule for eighteen months. He calls me if he's heading out for a run. He calls me if he's thinking about eating something new. He's petrified of WADA.'

'The anti-doping guys?'

'Too right,' Brown says. 'They can knock on your door any time, demanding urine and blood.'

'Gilmore's clean, though?' Paz asks.

'You bet. But if you're not there when they show up, the world thinks you're a cheat for the rest of your career. Especially when you're as good as Tim.'

He sighs, and I wonder if he's slept at all.

'Can you get us into Gilmore's room?' I ask.

He nods.

'He's sharing with Oscar Ryan, the hammer-thrower. Have you heard of him?'

I shake my head.

'You will have, by the end of these Games,' Hunter Brown says and, for a moment, he smiles. 'Anyway, Oscar'll let us in.'

'Well,' Paz says. 'Let's go and wake him up.'

THE LIFT IS TIGHT and intimate, and I get the feeling Hunter Brown wants to tell me something. Before he gets a chance, the doors open and we're out into a long, straight corridor. The place smells of fresh paint and new carpet.

We walk down the corridor until Brown stops outside a door and says, 'This is it.'

A brooding hulk of a guy opens the door and fills most of the frame. He looks as though he could crush a man without breaking a sweat, and without losing much sleep over it, either. I assume he's Oscar Ryan, but I never find out because he gives the slightest nod of recognition to Hunter Brown while scowling at all three of us, and then melts back into the darkness and disappears into his room.

'There's something you need to know about Tim Gilmore,' Brown says as he leads us through the gloom. 'He is not in a great place right now.'

The room is square, and one wall is taken up by a picture window, while another is covered with white high-gloss kitchen units. The floor is wooden and scuffs noisily, and there is flat-screen

TV stuck to one of the magnolia walls. A single bulb, underneath the extractor hood above the cooker, lights the entire scene. I fall into one of the sofas opposite the Aussie team coach. The dim light casts long shadows and gives his eyes a hooded and careworn appearance.

'What do you mean – "he's not in a great place"?'

Brown sighs.

'He has a media image as the all-Australian hero. He struggles to live up to it. This is the best chance he's had of winning Olympic gold.'

'He's feeling the pressure?'

'Too bloody right.'

Behind the coach, Paz is skulking around the place, picking up bottles of protein supplements and boxes of pasta. Looking for clues.

She stops pacing and sits down next to me on the sofa. I ask her if she's found anything interesting and she shakes her head.

'Gilmore's the messy one,' Brown says as I gaze across the unwashed plates and unfolded sports kit littering the room. There's a book on the sofa with its spine broken and a scrap of paper marking the point Gilmore had reached. I find myself wondering if he'll ever finish it.

Then I notice writing on the bookmark. I pull it out and turn it over in my fingers, before handing it to Paz. It's a phone number written on top of a supermarket receipt.

'Mobile phone,' Paz says. 'Could be something.'

'That's a local supermarket,' I say, 'so he's only recently written the number down. Who does he need to contact in Rio that isn't already on his phone?'

I pull out my own phone. I dial the number and listen to it ringing out.

THE MARACANÃ STADIUM IS an imposing fortress, and there is excitement on the faces of everyone bustling past me, as I wait outside and soak up the atmosphere.

Officially I'm on duty tonight, supervising the VIP section. In reality, I have front-row seats for the show. It's a thank-you from the city for four decades of service. Juliana is holding my hand and I can feel the excitement pulsing through her. She's proud of me. She told me as much as she was straightening my jacket before we left. Paz is on my other arm clutching Felipe, her young boy, to her side.

'Keep your eyes open tonight,' she tells him. 'You'll still remember all of this when you're as old as Carvalho.'

Paz winks at me and flashes that toothpaste-advert smile. We've been working on the Gilmore case all day, without much joy, and we're both keen to shake off the day and enjoy ourselves. The air is crackling with anticipation and pride. The biggest show on earth has arrived in Rio. I think of Igor Morales, a friend of my dad's when he was alive, and now a lifelong friend of mine. We play dominoes together on Friday nights and he tells me stories of watching Uruguay winning the World Cup in 1950, with two hundred thousand people crammed inside the Maracanã Stadium.

'Hold on to Felipe,' I tell Paz. With every step we take towards the stadium, the crowd gets tighter.

'Way ahead of you.'

I grip Juliana's hand and push forward into the crowd. People are smiling and joking as they shuffle slowly forward. It takes us fifteen minutes to get into the VIP section. Felipe is wide-eyed with excitement. Our seats have been covered in sky-blue leather, in time for the Games, and cup-holders have been built into the armrests. I guess Igor Morales wouldn't recognise the place.

'Will you watch Felipe? I'm going to get drinks,' Paz shouts above the roar of the crowd, which seems close to fever pitch before the ceremony has even begun.

The stretched-plastic roof feels like canvas above us, as if the whole crowd is cocooned in a Bedouin tent as the last of the daylight begins to fade and the first of the stars emerge. Music pumps through the air, and the giant screens hanging from gantries high above our heads race through the superhuman achievements of previous competitors. It is visceral. And intoxicating. I turn and kiss Juliana's cheek, same as I've done for the past forty years, and feel the warmth of her skin.

'Break it up, lovebirds.' Paz smiles as she returns through the crowd. 'I got hot dogs.'

Suddenly the crowd erupts as, twenty yards to our right, the presidential party arrives. We are the *almost-VIPs* – the security-approved buffer between the real VIPs and the cheap seats. Felipe spots the President and points in astonishment.

With perfect orchestration, the stadium fades to black, the instant the President takes her seat. Stars peer down curiously through the yawning centre of the roof and the music stops, replaced by the whistles of the crowd. Then silence. One last breath before the madness.

When it happens, it is a roar and a cacophony. The first boom of fireworks shakes the blood in my arteries, and there's an explosion of colour and fire. The music returns, driving and insistent. Hundreds of musicians suddenly appear from every tunnelled entrance and flood onto the arena surface, coming together to play an ear-shattering fanfare. Juliana is inching forward to get the best possible view. The entire sky is ablaze, and now, behind the musicians, hundreds of athletes are streaming into view. They move in teams, bathed in restless and garish lights, swirling around the edge of the field.

Flags start appearing on the screens. Afghanistan, Antigua and Saudi Arabia all join the parade. As we watch, the Australian flag flutters onto the giant screens and a section of green-and-gold-clad spectators cheer far away behind us. The camera follows the flag down to its bearer, a man in his mid-twenties with a square jaw, broad shoulders and tight bronze skin. I stare at the huge screen, transfixed and disbelieving, because the man holding the flag is Tim Gilmore. His eyes have a far-away quality and he is wearing earphones. He's chewing gum and staring straight ahead. I glance over towards Paz, who looks confused.

'What the hell?'

I shrug and she frowns.

'Easiest missing-person case we've ever solved, I guess.'

I glance back up to the screen, but Gilmore has gone. Instinctively I move forward from my seat and push up against the waist-high metal bars separating us from the arena. An official heads towards me, but I show him my badge and he backs off. Instinct tells me to keep my badge out, chained around my neck, as I sense Paz on my shoulder. We search out the Australian team and, in the distance, I can see Gilmore leading them towards us in the parade. Fifty yards away, maybe. He is holding the flag in one hand, and in the other he has his javelin, symbolically held aloft as he leads his team forward.

'Is that even allowed?' Paz asks.

I shrug again, as my stomach starts to tighten slightly. As we watch, Gilmore hands his flag to a teammate. I can see that it's Oscar Ryan, the hammer-thrower. Gilmore turns and looks our way and, with his javelin held aloft, steps away from his team and begins to jog slowly against the flow of the parade, directly towards us.

Gilmore picks up pace, heading for the presidential party with his javelin held aloft. All at once, I am convinced something terrible is about to happen. I see his arm pull back into a throwing position, and finally the President and the crowd around her see the danger. Gilmore arches his back, ready to sling his javelin forward.

A woman next to me screams, but the music pumps on. Suddenly I'm aware of the gun in my hand and the cold metal of the trigger on my finger. I do not choose to fire; I don't make any conscious decision. It just happens. Three times, straight into the chest of Tim Gilmore. He twists and falls to the floor, and I watch a security team spill out from the VIP section and drag his lifeless body away out of sight. A huddle of nearby athletes watch on, horrified, but soon they are swept away in the tide of others. My gunshots were lost in the explosion of fireworks, and the TV cameras are pointing elsewhere. The show goes on.

'Jesus Christ!' Paz says, and I turn to find her right next to me, badge out and gun drawn. 'What the hell just happened?'

Oscar Ryan, the hammer-thrower, is walking against the tide of athletes and is staring straight at us. A tight scrum of security guards is moving the President away from the arena, but the parade continues and the fireworks still explode and the lights continue to flash. And the only thing that has changed in the world is that I've got a sinking feeling that Tim Gilmore is dead.

ABOUT A MINUTE AFTER Tim Gilmore hits the floor, a group of Policia Militar arrive and bundle Paz and me towards the exit. Paz twists back in time to see Juliana grab hold of Felipe, and then falls into line with me and the boots and the berets, because there is no point fighting them. Nobody says anything until we are deep enough into the bowels of the Maracanã that the fireworks are no more than muffled thuds and the crowd is a distant memory.

'He's Tim Gilmore,' I say, looking at the tall military policeman leading the way.

He stops walking and turns round to face me, his eyes shining with a potent cocktail of machismo and adrenalin.

'He went missing yesterday,' I tell him. 'We've been investigating since five a.m. this morning.'

The tall commander inches closer to me and puts a rough hand on my chest.

'This is *my* stadium,' he says. 'My jurisdiction. And I didn't ask you to talk, old-timer.'

The commander is dressed for action, with his black protective vest over navy combat gear. He has a gun strapped to one thigh and another across his chest. None of it impresses me. I'm wondering whether Tim Gilmore is dead or alive, and this guy is worrying about the size of his jurisdiction. I ignore his guns and grandeur and look him in the eye.

'I don't need anyone's permission to speak.'

'You sure as hell need my permission to shoot in a restricted area,' he says, jutting his chin and getting in my face to emphasise the point. 'You're lucky we didn't fire back.'

He pushes at my chest to see if I'll yield. I don't. Instead, I slowly bring my hand up and take hold of his thumb. He is twenty years younger than me, but one of nature's laws says that if you bend a man's thumb back, he has only two options, regardless of how tough he is. Either he moves with the pressure, or he waits for the bone to snap. Moving with the pressure goes something like this: you move your wrist to compensate for the pressure on your thumb. Then you're forced to move your elbow to compensate for your wrist; your shoulder for your elbow; your hips for your shoulder; and eventually you're on the floor in front of all the men in your unit.

I see reality dawning in his eyes as he begins to yield to my pressure. Yielding to the *old-timer*. Our eyes are still locked when I sense the atmosphere change. A new team of tough guys break through the circle of men who are surrounding me and Paz. From within the new group the President emerges without breaking her stride. I let go of the commander's thumb and he turns to face her.

'Ma'am,' he says, his voice laced with authority and crackling with ambition.

She comes straight to the point.

'Who was the guy with the spear?'

'We don't know for sure.'

'His name is Tim Gilmore,' I say, and everybody turns and looks at me. 'He's the Australian team captain. He was reported missing overnight by his coach, and we have been actively looking for him since about five a.m. this morning. His coach was concerned because he's been suffering from some anxiety issues.'

'And who are you?' the President asks.

'He's the guy who shot the athlete,' the tall commander says. 'Don't worry, we're dealing with him.'

The President raises an eyebrow.

'You're *dealing* with him?'

'Ma'am, we have strict regulations that say we should shoot as a last resort. Two billion people around the world are watching on TV, and our protocols are designed to protect Brazil's image and reputation.'

The President shakes her head.

'Your protocols nearly had me skewered.'

She turns to me and takes hold of my hand.

'What's your name?'

'Carvalho.'

She turns away from me and holds my hand aloft, as if I'm Barão do Amazonas, the hero from classical legend, returning from Riachuelo. I'm not comfortable with it at all.

'This man is a hero,' she says. 'Anyone who treats him differently will answer to me, understand?'

She gives the commander a barbed look, before settling her gaze back on me.

'Can I do anything for you?'

'I want to know what happened to Tim Gilmore. He's a young man and he's trained his whole life to be here.'

The presidential eyebrow rises in anticipation as she waits for the commander to speak.

'Gilmore's dead.'

'There you go,' the President says. 'You did your job, Carvalho. And if you hadn't, then I would be dead right now. Whatever happened was his choice, not yours.'

Then she's gone. I feel sick to my stomach, thinking about Gilmore lying dead in some other corridor nearby, while most of the people outside have no idea what has happened. I've shot plenty of people, but this one certainly doesn't make me feel good.

'Get a statement from Oscar Ryan,' I tell the commander. 'He was right next to Gilmore. Find out what he said.'

The Policia Militar melt away without an apology and I am left facing Paz across the corridor.

'Come on,' she says in a low voice. 'Let's get home. At least we can beat the crowds.'

JAMES PATTERSON
BOOKSHOTS
OUT THIS MONTH

CHASE: A MICHAEL BENNETT THRILLER

A man falls to his death in an apparent accident. But why does he have the fingerprints of another man who is already dead? Detective Michael Bennett is on the case.

LET'S PLAY MAKE-BELIEVE

Christy and Marty just met, and it's love at first sight. Or is it? One of them is playing a dangerous game – and only one will survive.

DEAD HEAT

Detective Carvalho is investigating the disappearance of a key athlete on the day of the opening ceremony of the 2016 Olympic Games. The case is about to take a deadly turn …

THE McCULLAGH INN IN MAINE

Chelsea O'Kane escapes to Maine to build a new life – until she runs into her old flame Jeremy Holland …

TRIPLE THREAT

Three pulse-pounding stories in one book! *Cross Kill*, *Zoo 2* and *The Pretender*.

THE PRETENDER (ebook only)

Logan Bishop is a thief living off a stash of stolen diamonds. But when his murderous ex-partner tracks him down, Logan could lose it all …

JAMES PATTERSON
BOOKSHOTS
COMING SOON

113 MINUTES

Molly Rourke's son has been murdered ... and she knows who's responsible. Now she's taking the law into her own hands.

THE VERDICT

A billionaire businessman is on trial for violently attacking a woman in her bed. No one is prepared for the terrifying consequences of the verdict.

THE MATING SEASON

Sophie Castle has been given the opportunity of a lifetime: her own wildlife documentary. But her cameraman, Rigg Greensman, is unmotivated ... and drop dead gorgeous.

ALSO BY JAMES PATTERSON

ALEX CROSS NOVELS
Along Came a Spider
Kiss the Girls
Jack and Jill
Cat and Mouse
Pop Goes the Weasel
Roses are Red
Violets are Blue
Four Blind Mice
The Big Bad Wolf
London Bridges
Mary, Mary
Cross
Double Cross
Cross Country
Alex Cross's Trial (*with Richard DiLallo*)
I, Alex Cross
Cross Fire
Kill Alex Cross
Merry Christmas, Alex Cross
Alex Cross, Run
Cross My Heart
Hope to Die
Cross Justice

THE WOMEN'S MURDER CLUB SERIES
1st to Die
2nd Chance (*with Andrew Gross*)
3rd Degree (*with Andrew Gross*)
4th of July (*with Maxine Paetro*)

The 5th Horseman (*with Maxine Paetro*)
The 6th Target (*with Maxine Paetro*)
7th Heaven (*with Maxine Paetro*)
8th Confession (*with Maxine Paetro*)
9th Judgement (*with Maxine Paetro*)
10th Anniversary (*with Maxine Paetro*)
11th Hour (*with Maxine Paetro*)
12th of Never (*with Maxine Paetro*)
Unlucky 13 (*with Maxine Paetro*)
14th Deadly Sin (*with Maxine Paetro*)
15th Affair (*with Maxine Paetro*)

DETECTIVE MICHAEL BENNETT SERIES
Step on a Crack (*with Michael Ledwidge*)
Run for Your Life (*with Michael Ledwidge*)
Worst Case (*with Michael Ledwidge*)
Tick Tock (*with Michael Ledwidge*)
I, Michael Bennett (*with Michael Ledwidge*)
Gone (*with Michael Ledwidge*)
Burn (*with Michael Ledwidge*)
Alert (*with Michael Ledwidge*)
Bullseye (*with Michael Ledwidge*)

PRIVATE NOVELS
Private (*with Maxine Paetro*)
Private London (*with Mark Pearson*)
Private Games (*with Mark Sullivan*)
Private: No. 1 Suspect (*with Maxine Paetro*)

Private Berlin (*with Mark Sullivan*)

Private Down Under (*with Michael White*)

Private L.A. (*with Mark Sullivan*)

Private India (*with Ashwin Sanghi*)

Private Vegas (*with Maxine Paetro*)

Private Sydney (*with Kathryn Fox*)

Private Paris (*with Mark Sullivan*)

The Games (*with Mark Sullivan*)

NYPD RED SERIES

NYPD Red (*with Marshall Karp*)

NYPD Red 2 (*with Marshall Karp*)

NYPD Red 3 (*with Marshall Karp*)

NYPD Red 4 (*with Marshall Karp*)

STAND-ALONE THRILLERS

Sail (*with Howard Roughan*)

Swimsuit (*with Maxine Paetro*)

Don't Blink (*with Howard Roughan*)

Postcard Killers (*with Liza Marklund*)

Toys (*with Neil McMahon*)

Now You See Her (*with Michael Ledwidge*)

Kill Me If You Can (*with Marshall Karp*)

Guilty Wives (*with David Ellis*)

Zoo (*with Michael Ledwidge*)

Second Honeymoon (*with Howard Roughan*)

Mistress (*with David Ellis*)

Invisible (*with David Ellis*)

The Thomas Berryman Number

Truth or Die (*with Howard Roughan*)

Murder House (*with David Ellis*)

NON-FICTION

Torn Apart (*with Hal and Cory Friedman*)

The Murder of King Tut (*with Martin Dugard*)

ROMANCE

Sundays at Tiffany's (*with Gabrielle Charbonnet*)

The Christmas Wedding (*with Richard DiLallo*)

First Love (*with Emily Raymond*)

OTHER TITLES

Miracle at Augusta (*with Peter de Jonge*)

BOOKSHOTS

Black & Blue (*with Candice Fox*)

Break Point (*with Lee Stone*)

Cross Kill

Private Royals (*with Rees Jones*)

The Hostage (*with Robert Gold*)

Zoo 2 (*with Max DiLallo*)

Heist (*with Rees Jones*)

Hunted (*with Andrew Holmes*)

Airport: Code Red (*with Michael White*)

The Trial (*with Maxine Paetro*)

Little Black Dress (*with Emily Raymond*)